Surprised by Joy

May Paddock

Cover Photo: May Paddock
Cover Design: Tom Stier

Edited by: Rosemary Ahearn

Website developed by Tom Stier

Visit the author website:
http://www.maypaddockt.com

ISBN: ISBN: 978-1-939980-16-8 (Kindle)
ISBN: 978-1-939980-17-5 (epub)
ISBN: ISBN: 978-1-939980-18-2 (Paperback)
ISBN: ISBN: 978-1-939980-19-9 (Audio)

Published by: WriteSpa Press

Version: 2018.03.26

In Memory of

Fred Paddock

Chapter One

Joan
Ipswich, Massachusetts
January 1992

Shivering, with snow numbing her ankles, Joan tipped a heavy planter near the front door of her cottage to find the key she'd hidden there three years before. With the key in her hand, she straightened up and waved to the taxi driver, who waved back before he pulled away. She opened the door and carried in her backpack and the bags of provisions and bottled water she'd bought when she got off the train.

Although the cottage was bleakly cold, it seemed to welcome her home. Joan rummaged in a closet and found a heavy jacket. She opened the door to the back porch and pulled firewood and kindling out from under a tarp. She emptied one of the grocery bags onto the kitchen table, tore the bag into pieces which she scrunched up for the first layer of a fire in the hearth. Once the kindling and then the wood caught, she sighed deeply. She was going to manage.

There was no electricity, so the furnace and water pump couldn't work. Her first stop after getting off the train at Ipswich had been the telephone company. They said they'd have her reconnected "in a day or two." She used a bucket as her toilet, and then put on boots to deposit its contents in the field beyond the garden, rinsing out the bucket with snow. That done, she straightened up and looked around. It had been years since she'd seen snow. She paused to take in the wonder of its gentle silent covering of everything.

The clouds were turning pink as the sun headed for the horizon. Joan went inside and made herself high tea — boiled eggs and bread and cheese which she ate sitting on the sofa, pulled up as close to the fire as was safe. As the light began to fade, she piled more wood near the fireplace, got blankets from all four beds, and made herself as comfortable as possible on the sofa with a candle and a copy of *Tristram Shandy*.

Each time the cold woke her up, she added more logs to the fire. At one point she needed to pee. She realized that she'd left the bucket outside. She lit her candle, found her boots and warm jacket and went out the kitchen door. The full moon lit up the wide snowy field beyond the garden. The stars seemed to be sending messages from her dead husband, Oscar, and his two daughters, "We're here! We're fine. Be at peace."

In the morning, the day was mild and sunny; the snow glinted and gleamed over the field and along every branch and twig. It was as though Oscar was winking at her. Breakfast was two more eggs, boiled in the same water from the night before. Then that water was used to make coffee, which she drank standing with her back to the fire.

Joan decided that the best way to get warm would be to take a walk up to the mansion at the top of the driveway. It was built in the style of a villa in Tuscany with pale pink plaster walls that shimmered in the light. The owners of the mansion lived there for a few months each year during fox-hunting and horse show season. Their five horses lived full time in the barn at the foot of the driveway. Behind the barn and alongside the long driveway to the mansion was a field fenced in with wooden boards and posts painted white.

The clouds skidded across the sky, letting the sun shine through intermittently. At the top of the driveway, Joan decided to turn left and walk through the snow into the woods behind the mansion. She found a deer trail that led to the bank of the wide and shallow Ipswich River. Its surface was frozen and translucent. A stream flowed visibly under the ice circling the protruding rocks. The sun glinted off the icy surfaces of river, rocks, and trees. As she stared, Joan felt Oscar, standing beside her. She stood as still as possible because although the sensation felt real, it also felt fragile, as though she could shatter it if she moved carelessly. She realized she was crying because the world in front of her began to disappear. Snow started to fall. Joan had forgotten her hat, and as the snow landed on the back of her neck and stuck to the tears on her face, Oscar's warmth withdrew. When it was completely gone, she turned to retrace her steps along the deer tracks that were rapidly disappearing, back to the mansion's driveway, and then home.

That afternoon the telephone company called. She was connected. Joan arranged with "Ipswich Taxi" for a ride into town the next morning so she could go to the bank, and then leave deposits at the fuel and electric companies. She was very much looking forward to a long hot shower in a warm bathroom.

Chapter Two

Seamus
Hudson, New York
January 1992

Seamus tripped on the top stair but managed to grab the handrail before he fell. He wasn't yet used to his prosthetic foot. As he stood in the doorway of the second-floor office, a woman with her back to him was sipping coffee and talking on the phone. "Listen, Jorge, I don't need an assistant, especially an ex-cop. You could at least have warned me. I'm telling you right now, if it doesn't work out, I'm not ... Oh, I think he's arrived. I'll get back to you."

She hung up the phone, turned her chair around, and stood up. Seamus caught his breath. Her dark skin color set off exquisite features surrounded by multiple tight braids that came down to her shoulders. She wore blue jeans and a bright red turtleneck sweater over her generously curved body. Seamus seldom noticed women's looks any more, but he thought this new supervisor of his was stunning. He stared at her instead of introducing himself. She finally said, "I'm assuming you're Sergeant Carroll. I'm Jasmine Brown."

"I'm Seamus Carroll, no longer a sergeant, and pleased to meet you. I gather you didn't know I was coming. Sorry to be a surprise."

She smiled in embarrassment, and said as they shook hands, "A good surprise I'm sure. Jorge tells me you speak Spanish. That should be very helpful. I think, though, that we won't tell anyone that you used to be a policeman. Our clients have not always been treated well by the police.

"Okay, we'll stick to the present," Seamus said, though he thought to himself that he'd give anything to go back in time and have his wife, Rose, alive again.

When they sat down, Jasmine said, "I don't know how much Jorge told you about Migrant Advocacy. Our goal is to register as many migrant farmworkers in the county as possible and help them obtain year-round work. Meanwhile we help with medical care etc., whatever we can do to make their lives easier. It's important to keep good data, so why don't you begin by reading our brochures and then entering the data from last week onto my computer."

"I know nothing about computers," Seamus said quickly.

"Didn't Jorge ask you about computers? I guess he was so pleased that you were bilingual that he forgot everything else. Well, I needed to learn about computers recently myself. Putting the data in is very straight forward. I'll show you."

Hours later, after Seamus had made every mistake a person can make as he types in columns of names and numbers, he pressed the "print" button, feeling like St. Michael after he'd conquered the dragon.

"It's almost lunch time," Jasmine announced. "Give yourself an hour, and then here's a map of the county with stars marking the farms we've yet to visit. Don't go near the main farmhouses; look for the dirt tracks leading back to the trailers. If anyone's home, get the outreach forms filled out. If the worker is illiterate, ask him or her questions and you fill it out. Tell them you're going to return some evening soon, to talk with the people who are working during the day. Did Jorge tell you about that? You're going to be the most help to me if you go out in the evenings. If there's nobody at home in the trailers, leave an English and Spanish brochure at the door, and go back some night as soon as you can. I'll see you here tomorrow morning. Good Luck."

It was a relief to get out of that office. Seamus stopped in the pub for a beer and wings, and then headed out. Once he got off Rte. 9, he looked for dirt roads near barns. Two of them became grassy tracks and then disappeared altogether. The third led to a trailer. Seamus used the rickety hand rail to pull himself up the metal stairs to knock at the door. A teenager opened it with a baby on her hip. Seamus greeted her in Spanish and asked if she'd be willing to talk with him for a few minutes about an organization called Migrant Advocacy. The teenager told him her name was Claudia, and she welcomed him inside as though he were the friend she'd been waiting for all afternoon. They sat at the table in the combination kitchen, living room and bedroom. Seamus told Claudia the little he knew about the Migrant Advocacy program and showed her the brochure in Spanish and the registration form. Claudia handed him the squirming baby and began to slowly read the brochure. Then she found a pen and carefully filled in the requested information on the form. Meanwhile the baby fell fast asleep on Seamus's lap and he remembered how Rose had always said he had a way with infants. "They know what a honey you are at heart," she'd said.

When Claudia handed him the form and took the baby back, she said, "It's a miracle you got Lalo to sleep. He's been teething something awful. He's my friend Ruby's baby. Ruby had a math test today, so she had to go to school. The daycare sent Lalo home yesterday because he has pink eye. Tomorrow I have a history exam, so Ruby will stay home with Lalo." She offered Seamus a coke. He said he'd prefer water. As she poured water from a large pitcher he looked around. There were two single beds against opposite walls. They each had two pillows and were covered by a blanket. There were no pillowcases or sheets. There was a plastic laundry basket on the floor next to one of the beds. The only decoration was a picture on the wall of Jesus pointing to a valentine-shaped heart on his chest. Claudia explained that she and Ruby and their husbands had arrived in November because her husband had heard of a job on someone's estate. That hadn't worked out, but a cousin had arranged with the owner of this farm to rent the trailer to the two families until April when the farm would have work for them. Meanwhile the men were working in a plastics factory in Hudson, and Claudia and Ruby were taking turns cleaning people's houses, going to school, and taking care of Lalo. School was difficult because neither of them could understand much English, but they were learning little by little.

Seamus told Claudia that he would be back one evening soon with more registration forms for her husband and friends. He added, "Perhaps I can help you and Ruby with your homework while your husbands fill out the forms."

Claudia beamed at him. "That would be a miracle," she said, as she lifted the baby to her shoulder and then stood to walk him to the door.

As he drove, in what he hoped was the right direction for Hudson, Seamus found himself singing "All You Need is Love," a song that his daughter, Caitlin, had taught him many years before.

Chapter Three

Maura
London, England
January 1992

Maura stared through a shop window at a Japanese maple made into a bonsai tree. Why, she asked herself, would someone turn a tree into a table decoration? Then the sun came out from behind a cloud, and instead of seeing the bonsai through the window, Maura saw her own reflection, and behind her someone who looked like Terrance, ardently kissing a woman she couldn't see.

Maura stood as still as possible. Terrance put an arm around the woman's waist, and they walked away. Maura could see enough to be sure it was her husband, but she could only see the woman's back. The woman was tall and thin, with dark hair piled high on her head. She wore a shimmery dress that showed every curve.

Early that morning, while the family was eating breakfast, someone had phoned Terrance. After breakfast, as Maura headed out to teach her first class, Terrance had said, "I have an audition this afternoon. I'll leave the boys off with Mum. Could you pick them up?"

"Of course," Maura said. "Congratulations!"

"I haven't got it yet, have I," he said with a smile, and surprised Maura by kissing her on the mouth.

"Yuck" said Toby, already a critic at age five.

"Bye, Mum," said Ben, two years younger.

As Maura entered her mother-in-law's apartment that afternoon, she saw a ball hit a lamp which she managed to grab before it fell. "Thank you, dear," Veronica said. "I've asked the boys not play with the ball in here, but…."

"We're sorry, Grandma," Toby said quickly.

"I know you try to be careful. There are some cookies and milk in the kitchen. Please eat them in there. I don't want spills on the rug."

"Have they been impossible?"

"They're good boys, the best in the world, but I think I'm getting a little too old to have them all day."

"All day? I thought Terrance was going to leave them here for an hour or two while he went to an audition."

"He didn't tell me where he was going, but he brought them here right after breakfast."

Maura could think of nothing to say to her dear and generous mother-in-law, so she kissed her on the cheek, and went to the kitchen where the boys were scarfing up cookies.

"Let's go. We've got about an hour for the park. Put your plates and cups in the sink. Thank Grandma for putting up with you and get your jackets."

Maura was grateful that Terrance wouldn't be home that evening. Between acting jobs, he worked as a bartender. In the past, the down times had been short. Now the stretches of unemployment were getting longer and more frequent.

When they got home from the park, the boys shared a bath while Maura made supper. After supper the three of them sat on Ben's bed while she read poems from "Now We Are Six," and they all recited "James James Morrison Morrison" by heart. When the boys were asleep, and the dishes done, Maura went to her study to prepare for the next day's classes. Around midnight Terrance knocked and came in without waiting for her response. He sat down on the guest bed without a word and looked at her.

"Did you get the part?" she asked after a moment or two of his silence.

"There wasn't any audition," he said, as though she were naive to think there had been.

Maura said nothing.

"I saw you Maura. I saw you in front of the plant store. And I know you saw me, me and Carlotta. The thing is, Maura, the thing is I don't think it's completely my fault that I'm not doing so well."

"What do you mean?"

"Acting has a lot to do with presentation. And when you

and I go somewhere, we don't look special. We used to, you know. You used to look outstanding before you put on weight with the boys. I wish you'd..."

"What are you talking about?" Maura interrupted.

"I think you're pulling me down, you and the boys really. I think I need to be on my own, or with someone like Carlotta, for people to see me as star material."

Maura stared at her husband. His once chiseled features were dulled — his face had become slightly doughy. He smiled at her now showing all his whitened teeth, as though she were a producer he was trying to impress. She forced back her tears, promising herself the freedom to cry all night once she'd gotten Terrance out of her study.

Chapter Four

Joan
Ipswich, Massachusetts
February 1992

Ipswich was covered by clouds heavy with snow. Over the weeks the sun appeared rarely and briefly. Cars and trucks drove past Joan's driveway fast or slowly, depending on the iciness of the road, but only one truck turned in. It was driven by a young man who fed the horses and mucked out their stalls. When the snow was high, he connected a plow to his truck and plowed the driveway all the way to the mansion. He and Joan waved at each other companionably if she happened to be outside, but his radio was turned so loud that they couldn't have heard each other if one of them had spoken.

During the last three years Joan had become accustomed to the heat and dust of Nicaragua the skies empty of clouds and the small village where she lived empty of trees that might give shade. She had traveled to Nicaragua as part of a delegation of Witness for Peace, whose mission was to bring American visitors to Nicaragua to investigate what was happening there and to prevent President Reagan from bombing the country.

On the night her delegation arrived in the village of Malpaisillo, the local Witness for Peace liaison knocked on people's doors asking if they could house a gringo for two weeks. Oscar Estrada welcomed Joan immediately, and introduced her to his three children. The oldest, Eloina, a nurse in the local clinic, quickly removed her things from her bedroom to make room for Joan.

Joan had studied Spanish during the six months before the trip, but it was quickly evident that she could neither speak nor understand more than a few words. Even so, as the days went by, she and the Estrada family began to enjoy each other. Oscar's teenage son, Juan, had taught himself songs by the Beatles although he didn't know what the lyrics meant. Juan and Joan sang them together, with others chiming in as the words became familiar. The family taught Joan a song about Nicaragua which she sang lustily without understanding all the words.

When Joan discovered the market in the center of town, she brought back a basket of vegetables each day. Oscar's daughter, Yeni, let Joan help her cook them on the wood stove with lots of gestures and laughter, and hand clapping when the dishes were presented for supper.

On the night before Joan was to return to the States, she and Oscar stayed up late, sitting out on the patio in rocking chairs, watching the stars shine down on them. After a long silence, Oscar took Joan's hand, and as they continued to stare up toward the heavens, he asked if Joan would consider doing him the great honor of marrying him. Joan found that she understood every word, and with no need to think at all, she said, "Yes."

Joan's first husband had died almost forty years before. She'd brought up their two daughters on her own. Her eldest was schizophrenic, and despite everything that hospitals and doctors, and Joan herself could do, her daughter had committed suicide. It was in the aftermath of Angelica's suicide that Joan had decided to join Witness for Peace.

About six months later, when Oscar's children told him they were leaving for the mountains to take part in the war against the Contras, Oscar decided he would have to go with them. He explained to Joan, "I can't have my children in harm's way up in the mountains without fighting beside them, old man though I am. Oscar suggested that Joan return to live in the States during the fighting, but Joan knew she wanted to remain in Malpaisillo, as close to her new family as possible. Once her family had left for the mountains, Joan was determined to become fluent in Spanish, so she spent a lot of time in the streets talking with her neighbors who patiently allowed her to make her way to the end of each sentence. With their help, she'd learned to even to joke in Spanish. Many of her neighbors had family members fighting in the mountains. They exalted together when the news was good and supported each other when they heard of casualties.

When peace was finally declared, Oscar and his two daughters remained in the mountains buried under makeshift graves. Oscar's son, Juan, returned to Malpaisillo eager to begin life anew. He told Joan, "My father helped me so much to study computers. I want to set up a store in his honor to repair and sell them." Joan wanted to help her only surviving stepchild in any way she could. Since she had no money to invest in a storefront, she decided to move back to the States, so Juan could set up his computer store in his father's house.

In Ipswich Joan wrote Juan every week asking for news. She wrote about the bright red cardinals and their more conservatively colored mates at the bird feeder, and the nut hatches that only ate what had dropped onto the ground. She described how the horses, when they were let out of the barn on mild days, raced around the field in pure delight and sometimes rolled in the snow with their legs kicking in the air. She began and ended each letter by asking how Juan was and if his business was getting off the ground, and would he please send her news.

Chapter Five

Seamus
Hudson, New York
February 1992

Seamus's daughter, Caitlin, managed a repertory theater company in Carleton, a small town in Upstate New York. Seamus decided to leave the Boston Police Department to live near her, but he did not want to live in a small town. He and Caitlin explored Hudson, a city about twenty minutes away from Carleton. They took walks along the river, visited a friendly Irish pub, and, after a few days, they found a studio apartment in the attic of a Victorian house near the train station. It was a large room with a kitchen along one wall, and a small bathroom. Three floor-to-ceiling windows made it bright and airy. The wooden stairs to the attic were steep, but they were sturdy and had a new railing.

Seamus and Caitlin were interviewed by the owner who looked to be in her fifties. She wore a silk blouse that showed some cleavage, tight jeans, and high heels. She told Seamus that she was a lawyer specializing in divorces. "This house is loot from my own messy divorce. I fixed up the attic for my daughter. But despite hearing her father and me fight like a couple of tom cats, she's getting married to someone she hardly knows, and moving to Alabama." After looking Seamus up and down, she continued, "Your daughter tells me you were a policeman. I'm here only on weekends. I'd appreciate having an ex-policeman as a tenant. If you like the apartment but think it's too pricey, I'm willing to take ten percent off the rent."

The lower rent, the Irish pub, and Caitlin's hopeful smile decided Seamus. "It's a deal," he said, as he held out his hand.

Seamus found a Latina bodega near the Hudson river. The first time he went in, a customer was complaining about the weather in Spanish. Seamus chimed in. It felt good to be speaking Spanish again. He had patrolled the streets of East Boston for many years and had gone to night school to learn Spanish to make himself a more effective policeman. The owners of the bodega, Señor and Señora Esposito, were from Colombia. They sold take-out meals as well as groceries. After the first visit, Seamus went there almost every evening to buy something for supper. The food was always good and went well with a Guinness or two.

Seamus drove to Carleton every Wednesday to meet Caitlin for brunch at a café above the bookstore on Main Street. They walked back to her theater, the Globe, in time for the matinee. Seamus had bought himself season tickets — two seats in the front row for the first Wednesday matinee of each play. Caitlin had urged him to buy two seats, "so you can bring your friends, Dad. Suggesting someone come to a play with you is a good ice breaker." The plays the Globe chose to perform were "on the cutting edge," according to Caitlin. Some had only one or two actors, like *Krapp's Last Tape* or *The Zoo Story*. Some seemed to Seamus to have too many actors, like *The Skin of Our Teeth*. But he watched them all, and, as he told Caitlin, found them "interesting."

On Sunday mornings Seamus walked a few blocks from his apartment to a Catholic church. He and Rose had been very active in their church in Boston and had become good friends with the priest, Father Brennan. The priest in Hudson mumbled the Mass so softly and rapidly that as Seamus complained to Caitlin "He might just as well be speaking in Latin. And his homilies are paraphrases of the Gospel reading in case anyone had slept through it. After Mass when I duly stand in line to shake hands with the priest he's always looking over my shoulder at whoever's behind me. I'm assuming people are drinking coffee and eating doughnuts somewhere after the service, but it's never mentioned.

"Dad, you can always come out to Carleton for Mass." Caitlin told him.

"If I did, would you come with me?"

"No, Dad, but I'd give you a bang-up breakfast afterwards."

"I'll think about it." Seamus had said. But they both knew

he wouldn't. Caitlin hadn't gone to church since she moved out of their house in Boston. It had made him and Rose very unhappy, although Father Brennan had encouraged them to not argue with her about it. "She has to follow her own path. She's a fine young woman and you have every reason to be proud of her."

When a check of Seamus's bounced at the bodega, Señora Esposito was graciousness itself. Seamus's embarrassment sent him the next day to the Department of Labor to find some work. Filling out the past employment form was quick. He'd joined the police force right out of high school. On the list of skills, he checked "Bilingual - Spanish." They didn't ask, but he could have also told them he was an excellent marksman. After a wait of half an hour or so, he was interviewed by a scruffy young man who stared silently at the form and then asked, "Are you fluent in Spanish?"

"I wouldn't have said so if I weren't."

The young man lowered his eyes at that and then said, "There's an opening with a group called Migrant Advocacy. They want someone who can interview Latino farmworkers."

"Interview them about what?"

"Don't know. Do you want the number?"

Seamus thought of his embarrassment the day before at the bodega, and said, "Yes, why not."

Although the job would be in Hudson, the interview took place in Albany. Señor Jorge Gomez, a genial middle-aged

Puerto Rican, talked to Seamus in rapid Spanish. "I think you'll be just right for the job. Your supervisor in the Hudson office will be Jasmine Brown. She's a nice woman, very nice and very intelligent. She and her husband worked as migrant farm workers themselves for sixteen years or more. She's good at what she does, very good. The only problem is that she doesn't speak a word of Spanish. And every year that goes by, there are more Latinos and fewer African Americans migrating from farm to farm. Your job is to see if you can get migrant farmworkers the education or training that will enable them to obtain year-round work. This traveling all over the country is hard on the families. The children attend three or four different schools each year, and then teachers describe them as ignorant because they're having trouble keeping up. I'm sorry you can't meet Jasmine before you start, but she's on vacation. I'm sure you'll make a great team."

Chapter Six

Maura
London, England
February 1992

Terrance told Maura that he and Carlotta had been lovers for months. "A guy can get lonely during the day," he explained. "I don't mind taking care of the boys, but they're not company. You know what I mean?"

She did know what he meant. His declaration made her feel suffocatingly lonely. It didn't help that Carlotta turned out to be a supermodel whose face smiled triumphantly at Maura from various magazine covers.

Jessica Schmidt, the head of the Philosophy Department at the U, found Maura crying in the bathroom one afternoon. She took Maura into her office, and Maura told her what had happened. After a few minutes of silence, Jessica said, "You probably know that my husband has also been unfaithful." This was common knowledge in the department, and Maura nodded silently. "I haven't had the courage to leave him. At least, not yet," Jessica added, "but my guess is that you would encourage me to do so if I were to ask for your advice. Am I right?"

Maura stared at her colleague in confusion.

"So, let's talk about you for a moment. Do you think you should leave Terrance?"

Maura forced herself to consider the question, and finally said, "Yes, but I can't. I've got my classes and…

Jessica interrupted her, "Where would you and the boys go?"

The idea of leaving London seemed strange, almost eerie, but then Maura thought of Carlotta's pretty face staring at her from the newsstands. "Well, I grew up in Boston. We could stay with my uncle until I found a job. But…"

Jessica interrupted her again. "We'll tell the Dean you have a family emergency in the States. I'll finish your classes for you and give you a rave reference."

Maura stared at her colleague. Jessica's decisiveness made Maura feel breathless. Finally, she asked, "Do you want to get rid of me?"

Jessica smiled ruefully and sat back in her chair. "Of course not. I'm sorry." After a moment when neither spoke, Jessica said, "I think I was trying to gain my own freedom by osmosis. I am sorry."

Maura leaned back in her chair as well. After a few minutes she asked, "Would you really take on my classes?"

"Sure, I'd enjoy doing that. My secretary could take on a lot of this administration stuff."

There was another long pause before Maura asked, "Would you be able to convince the Dean that I had to leave because of the family? Otherwise I'd be breaking my contract."

"You're not breaking your contract if you arrange with me to take your classes. And, your family *is* why you're leaving. If you decide to," she added quickly. After a minute she continued, "I can say from experience that a woman who sticks with a philandering husband pretty soon feels like a doormat. And that's not good for their children."

"A doormat." Maura let that description rattle around inside her for a while. Jessica looked down and began to mark and shuffle papers on her desk.

After about ten minutes of only the sound of the papers and a scratch of the pen, Maura stood up very straight, interrupted Jessica's desk work to shake her hand, and say, "Thank you, thank you very much. Can you start taking the classes on Monday? I'll send you my syllabus."

Jessica stood up and came around from behind the desk. "I wish you all the luck in the world. Please keep in touch. I think you're going to be my inspiration!"

"Thank you for everything." They hugged long and hard, and Maura left without looking back.

Terrance seemed thrilled by Maura's news, "Boston sounds

like a wonderful idea, darling. It's important for the boys to know where you grew up and to meet your relatives. I'll tell everyone that your uncle needs you. In fact, I'm sure he does need you, since your aunt died. I think I'm in line for a good role in a juicy soap-opera. I'll send you a bunch of money if I get it. Meanwhile take half of our savings. You deserve it." Maura bit her lip to keep her fury to herself, and to let it strengthen her resolve.

The next afternoon Maura told Veronica her plans. Veronica had been more like a mother than a mother-in-law to Maura. She sobbed through her tears, "I don't think Terrance would have done this if his father were still alive. I'll miss the three of you unspeakably."

"We'll miss you too, unspeakably," Maura told her. "And wherever we are, we'll want you to join us whenever you can." After a moment she added, "And if you can't come to the States, I'll do what I can so that the boys can visit you here."

Terrance went with them in the taxi to Heathrow Airport. He gave Maura a quick peck on the cheek. Then he squatted down a little creakily and hugged the boys to him saying, "Take good care of your mother now. I'm counting on you." The boys nodded solemnly, then looked at Maura in confusion. She wanted to knock Terrance off his haunches, but instead said, "Off we go!

Chapter Seven

Joan
Ipswich
March 1992

Joan's life began to settle into a rhythm. After breakfast, when it wasn't snowing or frigid, she made herself leave the warm cottage and head up the driveway toward the mansion. Sometimes the branches of the trees were sheathed with ice and looked like jewels. Other mornings when the ice had melted, the bare trees took on a different beauty as their dark curves, straight lines, bulges and crevices made extraordinary designs in contrast to the grey sky. At times, the trees seemed to be dancing with each other or having conversations back and forth across the driveway. Behind the trees, orange and red bittersweet roamed along the bushes that separated the driveway from the fields.

In the afternoons she sometimes walked along the road. She liked the old mossy stone walls, now capped with snow, that had been created by hand by early farmers and were miraculously still standing. There were hardly any cars on the road, and no other walkers.

   During the daylight hours she almost reveled in her solitude. She sometimes thought, or imagined, she couldn't tell which, that Oscar walked beside her along the road or up the driveway to the mansion and through the woods to the river. Nights were another experience altogether. Sometimes she felt she could drown in her loneliness. In the evenings she read *Walden* very slowly, savoring Thoreau's images. He seemed to be promising her that if she could care enough about the details of nature, the veins of a leaf, the paths made by ice melting on a hillside, the changing colors of the river, if she could care enough about the natural beauty around her, her loneliness, like his, would dissipate.

Joan finally received a letter from Malpaisillo, but it was not from Juan. The envelope was from the Mayor's office. The letter was written by his secretary, Maria Nuñez, an old friend of Oscar's. The letter was written in formal Spanish as though Maria wanted to be sure that Joan understood every word.

   Dear Joan,
   I send you greetings from all of us and hope that you and your family are well.
   I am filled with sorrow about what I must tell you. Juan has had to leave Malpaisillo. A member of a Mexican drug cartel insisted that Juan give him a computer in exchange for "protection for the store." Juan refused, saying he hadn't fought and watched his family and

friends die around him to be frightened by a bully. When the man attempted to grab the computer, Juan hit him. The man was splayed out on the floor for a few minutes while Juan waited, hoping he would get up and leave all in one piece. Finally, he did, but as he left he said, 'That's the last time you'll ever touch anyone.'

When the Mayor heard about this, he was very concerned because he had heard stories about this cartel. He obtained a tourist visa and some money for Juan and told him, 'If your father were here he would say that you need to leave the country immediately until this blows over. Since your father has given his life for the country, I need to say it for him. We will inform your stepmother about what has happened, but it would be better if you do not try to find her in the States. This cartel is like an octopus; we don't know how far it reaches. God forbid they take their anger out on her.'

Juan left Malpaisillo immediately, locking up his house and leaving his computers in our care.

He sends you his love and asks for your prayers. He asks that you do not contact his friends here, and he does not plan to contact you in the States. He wants to keep you all safe.

I send you my love as well. We are praying for him, and I will let you know if I have more information. Please do not telephone us about this though, because we are almost certain that someone is listening to our calls.

With all best wishes,

Maria Nunez

After reading the letter several times, Joan felt as though she were turning into ice. She quickly made a fire in the hearth. Once it was blazing, she stood in front of it rubbing her hands together as though she were a homeless person trying to get warm at a fire in a garbage can. She realized she couldn't continue this journey of grieving Oscar and his daughters, and worrying about Juan, on her own. She had to call her daughter Sarah.

Sarah lived in upstate New York only a few hours away, but Joan had felt the need to be completely alone for a while. She had not wanted to talk about Oscar and his children or her decision to leave Nicaragua. She'd felt the need to catch up with herself in her grief and her precipitous leaving of the country she had come to love. Now, though, in the crisis of Juan's fleeing Nicaragua, Joan found that she couldn't bear carrying the worry about him alone. She needed to confide in her family.

Sarah answered on the first ring, "Mom, you sound so close!"

"I am, dear, I'm in Ipswich."

"In Ipswich?"

"Yes, it's a long story. I needed to be incommunicado for a while."

"Incommunicado from us?"

"It's hard to explain, but..."

"Oh, Mom," Sarah interrupted, "I'm sure you had your reasons. But can you imagine how frightened I would have been if I'd called the Mayor's office and been told you were no longer in Malpaisillo? I wouldn't even know how to ask whether they meant you'd left or had died!"

"Oh, Sarah, I am sorry."

"Well, anyway, welcome back. I'm thrilled you're safe. Can you come visit? Or do you still need to be on your own? Listen, Mom," she went on before Joan could answer, "I've got to go. I've got to pick up Kari from dance class. We'll talk later. Glad you're back, very glad," and she hung up before Joan could tell her about Juan.

That evening Sarah's husband, Joe, called. "I'm talking with you in Spanish," he said, "because I'm surrounded by your loving family and I want to give us some privacy. They think I'm showing off, which of course I may be. I want to tell you how happy we are that you're back, and how sorry we are about Oscar. I'm so glad I met him and saw how happy you were together."

"Yes," Joan said, speaking in Spanish as well. "He liked you too. I'm very glad you knew him, even just a little."

"The most important thing is that we'd love to have you visit us as soon as you feel ready. Sarah is feeling unhappy about being grumpy about your wanting to be incommunicado. Also, I want to tell you that your Karmann Ghia awaits you. We only need one car now since we're living on the Academy campus. I'm taking your car in tomorrow to have it inspected and tuned up. So, see you soon, Joan. Here's Sam."

"Grandma?"

"Hello Sam."

"Grandma, I mean *Abuelita, yo te amo.*"

"And I love you Sam. And I look forward to seeing you."

"Come soon, Grandma, I have lots of things to show you."

"I will dear."

"Here's Kari. Good-bye, I mean, *hasta luego.*"

"*Hasta luego*, Sam. Your accent is perfect."

"Grandma?"

"Hello Kari. How are you Sweetheart?"

"I'm good. I'm doing ballet."

"That's wonderful."

"Can you come and watch me?"

"Definitely. I look forward to it."

"Goodbye, Grandma. I love you."

"I love you too, Kari. Please let …" but she heard a click.

Later that night Joan called Sarah back and told her about Juan.

"I'm so sorry Mom." After a moment she went on. "Listen, I have a colleague at the Globe whose father is an ex-policeman and he speaks Spanish. Maybe he can help."

Chapter Eight

Seamus
Hudson, New York
March 1992

One afternoon Seamus mistakenly deleted a lot of data from Jasmine's computer. He expected to be fired there and then, but Jasmine was too busy attempting to retrieve what Seamus had deleted to speak to him after her exclamation of horror and fury. Forty minutes later when she found and retrieved the data, she sat back in her chair and sighed with relief. "You are never again to touch my computer for any reason whatever. Is that understood?"

"Yes, indeed," Seamus said. "I can't tell you how sorry I am."

"Words would have done you no good at all if I hadn't been able to find that stuff." After she stared at Seamus in silence for a minute or so, she said, "Here's what we'll do. You'll be on a new schedule. You'll work every evening, including weekends when necessary, and you'll make all the appointments with job interviews and doctors etc. and you'll do all the transporting. On Fridays you'll come into the office with a written report of everything you've done and the hours you worked. Agreed?"

"Agreed. And thank you. I am sorry."

Before the accident, Seamus's favorite shift with the Boston Police had been late nights. The accident had happened almost four months before. Seamus had been celebrating Thanksgiving with his daughter, Caitlin, in Carleton. He'd been driving back to Boston that night, remembering happier Thanksgiving celebrations when his wife, Rose, was alive. He saw an old man trying to change a tire and pulled over to the side of the road to help him. As Seamus knelt to get the jack in place, a car swerved too close and drove over his foot. Instead of settling for a desk job after forty-five years of patrolling the streets, Seamus had decided to retire and move nearer to Caitlin.

Seamus visited the farmworkers' trailers in the evenings. If it was a trailer for single men, there would be eight or nine of them cooking supper, drinking beer, and taking turns in the shower. What amazed Seamus was how friendly they were. Whether he'd been there before or not, they greeted him as though he were a friend they were glad to see. Many of them had a tough time reading the brochures and couldn't fill in the forms Seamus brought. They had left school after a year or two to help earn money for their families. They'd been working ever since and sending money back home to various countries in Central America so that their families could pay their rent and have enough to eat. Some of the older men, men in their fifties, who were illiterate themselves, had children or grandchildren that they were putting through school and even college by their work, although they were never able to visit them. They were filled with pride at how well their families were doing back home even though they never saw them. Seamus had felt sorry for himself since Rose's death. Now he realized he had a lot to learn from these men who didn't get to see their families for decades.

Once they'd filled out the registration forms, Seamus asked them if there was anything he could do for them. Sometimes they told him about physical problems — the long hours of work were hard on their bodies. There was an Urgent Care Clinic in Hudson where he could take them. Often, they wanted his help in writing to their families. They would dictate their letters to him and Seamus learned through these letters of the struggles the men and their families were having because of their long separations and because of the problems of unemployment and gang violence and lack of drinking water in their home countries. Seamus brought writing paper and stamped envelopes with him on his visits. His job was to help seasonal farm workers find year-round work, but most of these men were accustomed to following the planting and harvesting seasons up and down the east coast, or between New England and Texas, and they were not eager to try something new. Jasmine had told Seamus to always put that offer forward, but to be helpful in any way he could.

Seamus was impressed by how well the men took care of each other. They encouraged each other to ask for his help. If he was taking someone to the clinic, that person would ask everyone else if there were errands they wanted him to run on the way back. The trailers were a very long walk from stores, and the workers took turns once a week being driven into town by the farm owner. Their responses to each other reminded Seamus of how it was in the police force. Policemen needed to trust each other to have their backs because the work was dangerous. These men needed to trust each other because their physical labor and the almost endless separation from their families were so debilitating.

Then there were the trailers that housed families, usually two or three families in each. The women got up before the men to make breakfast and tortillas by hand for everyone to take to work. They then got the children ready for day care or school, and everyone left for work at the same time. In the evenings, when Seamus visited, the women oversaw bathing the kids and making the supper. They tried hard not to get in each other's way as they took turns in the one bathroom, at the one stove, and the one table that could seat only some of them at a time. Everyone was exhausted from their long hours of work and Seamus was impressed by how gracious they were with each other as well as with him. Rose had been a teacher in a parochial school. She had sometimes invited the children to their house on Saturdays to help them with their homework. Trying to follow in her footsteps, Seamus sometimes sat at the table with the older kids after supper to explain homework assignments. The children went to three or four schools each year as their families followed the harvests. And the teachers ignored them, unless they were discipline problems, knowing that they would be moving on in a few months.

When Seamus talked to the families about getting year-round work, the mothers and children sometimes looked a little wistful, but generally the adults agreed with each other that it was good to follow the harvest since they knew how to eke out a living that way.

There was one part of his job that made Seamus uncomfortable. That was taking pregnant ladies to their prenatal appointments. He had tried to convince Jasmine that he could teach her all the Spanish words she would need for these appointments, but her answer had been clear, "You've been hired as my assistant only because you know how to speak Spanish, so speak it."

The women themselves didn't seem to mind Seamus being in on their conversations with the doctors. He stayed outside during the examinations themselves. The women and their husbands wanted him to be with them during the actual births. He stayed up near the mother's head and interpreted as the doctors and nurses told them what to do. Sometimes he'd be holding a younger sibling or two to keep them out of the way. The births often happened in the middle of the night. Seamus was always on call. The hospital would call him if the workers didn't have a phone. As a policeman he'd seen emergency births, sometimes after the mother had experienced trauma. But these births in the hospital, with the mothers often praying through their labor pains, and the siblings and fathers expectant and joyful, these births, Seamus felt, were celebrations of the miracle of life itself.

Chapter Nine

Maura
Cambridge, Massachusetts
March 1992

Once above the clouds, both boys fell fast asleep. When they arrived at the Boston airport, they took a taxi to Cambridge where Olivia, a friend of Maura's from high school, had an apartment. Before leaving London, Maura had called her uncle and was told that his number had been disconnected. Then she called Olivia who'd said, "It will be lovely to see you and to meet the boys, but I'm actually not home much. I'm more or less living with a guy in Somerville."

She wasn't home when they arrived, but she'd left a welcoming letter and a refrigerator full of food.

The next morning Maura and the boys took the subway to Boston. Maura had lived with her Uncle Seamus and Aunt Rose for almost two years after her father had been killed trying to protect bystanders during a shoot-out. Their house was on a block of brick houses with bay windows and stoops leading up to the front doors. Maura and the boys climbed the stoop to the front door and knocked. An elderly nun opened the door. Before Maura could say anything, the nun said, "Come in. Come in. Come in and get warm."

Once in the hall, Maura said, "We're looking for my uncle, Seamus Carroll." When the nun didn't respond, Maura wondered if she was a nurse, and asked a little hesitantly, "Is he alright?"

When the nun still didn't respond, Maura turned toward the stairs to go up to his bedroom. The nun stopped her by saying, "We're not allowed to tell anyone the names of our residents."

"But my uncle owns this house!" Maura almost shouted, half hoping that her uncle would hear her and come rushing downstairs to greet them.

The nun stood her ground despite Maura's outburst. In fact, she took a step towards her rather than away. "I don't know anything about the owner of the house. This is a shelter for women and children seeking refuge."

Maura stared at the nun in confusion and felt Toby and Ben take hold of her hands. After a moment the nun continued, speaking more gently, "Sometimes mail comes here that isn't for us. When that happens, I give it to Father Brennan. He's at the church five doors down. Perhaps he can tell you about your uncle."

Maura was grateful for being told where to go next in this

whirl of confusion. She mumbled, "Thank you Sister" and was about to turn away, when she heard Toby repeat, "Thank you," and saw him hold out his hand. Maura was about to apologize to the nun and explain to Toby that nuns don't shake hands, but this nun obligingly stretched out her hand to shake Toby's and then Ben's. The boys beamed. "Thank you again," Maura said, as they went back out into the cold.

The large heavy front door of the church was unlocked. When her eyes adjusted to the dimness inside, Maura saw a sign on an open door to the left that said, "Office." A grey-haired priest was reading at a desk covered with piles of books. He looked up as they stood in the doorway, smiled warmly, and said, "Hello! Come on in and sit down and tell me how I can help you."

They sat in the three chairs that faced the desk and Maura said, "Father, my uncle Seamus Carroll lived five doors down from here. We've just come from his house, but...."

"Are you Maura Trowbridge?"

"Yes, I am. Is Uncle Seamus alright?"

"Right as rain, right as rain, and won't he be happy to see you and to meet these little ones here! I'll give you his phone number," he continued as he spun a little wheel of cards. As he handed her a piece of paper with the information he said, "Your uncle is very proud of you. An MA in Philosophy, I think he said, the first in the family. He's also told me what a hero your father was. I'm sorry you lost him so young, but I can see that you've made great strides even so." As he talked, he stood up, as did Maura and the boys. "Shall we pray together?" Father Brennan asked.

"I would appreciate that," Maura said.

The priest raised his arms over their heads, "May God rain down blessings on Maura, Tobias, and Benjamin, and on their uncle Seamus. May we all learn how to discern God's will at every turning point in our lives. And may we be mindful that God is always ready to help, to console, and to guide us on every step of our journey. We pray this in the name of the Father, the Son and the Holy Spirit, Amen

Chapter Ten

Joan
Carleton, New York
March 1992

It was late in the afternoon when Joan got off the bus in Carleton. The sun had come out from behind the clouds as if it wanted to shine on everything before sinking below the horizon. Her family stood there in the bright sun light and she suddenly felt exceedingly glad that she'd come. She thought her daughter, Sarah, looked rather like Audrey Hepburn. Her brown hair was cut short, and she was still slim with a dancer's posture. Joan's grandson, Sam, wore his blond hair long, and pushed his bangs out of his eyes with a gesture that made him look older than his thirteen years. He was holding Bruce, Joan's old tom cat that her grandchildren had been taking care of while she was in Nicaragua. Joe, her son-in-law, looked professorial with horn-rimmed glasses and a greying beard. He had his arm around Sarah, who snuggled against him. Their eight-year old-daughter, Kari, had the upright posture of her mother, and her father's dark curly hair. She held a large cardboard sign with a rainbow of many colors over the text, 'Hola Grandma!'

For a moment, Joan felt self-conscious about her own looks. She'd lost weight during the fighting in Nicaragua, so her clothes from before were now too large. Her grey hair was in a long braid, and she had on a skirt that she'd made from a pair of Oscar's pants, topped by one of his work shirts. These were her comfort clothes, but they were not becoming. Her family, on the other hand, in woolen sweaters, winter vests, and corduroys or jeans, all looked exactly right. She forgot all this as soon as she began to hug them. She was home.

The next morning Sarah took Joan to a consignment store where she bought some new clothes. Then Sarah took her mother to her hairdresser who cut Joan's hair to just above her shoulders. Joan smiled into the mirror. She looked pretty good, she thought, for seventy-three.

As they left the hairdresser's, Joan said to Sarah, "I feel as though I'm here now."

"What do you mean?"

"I mean here in the States. Being with all of you and, now, thanks to you, looking more northern and contemporary, makes me feel more solidly here. Until now I've still had one foot in Nicaragua."

"I'm glad, Mom."

That afternoon Joan walked to the local library to meet with Seamus Carroll, the father of Sarah's colleague. He was sitting at a picnic table outside the library. She was almost sure it was him. He looked to be about her age. He sat very straight, smoked a cigarette and stared at her as she walked toward the library. Joan changed her direction and walked toward him, "Are you Mr. Carroll?"

"Yes indeed. Mrs. Estrada, I take it." He stood up and they shook hands. "If my cigarette doesn't bother you I was wondering if we could continue our conversation out here. My daughter, Caitlin, tells me you have a concern that I might be able to be helpful with."

"No, your cigarette doesn't bother me at all. I'm glad to stay out in the sun. Isn't it wonderful that spring has finally come?" When they sat down on the bench, she pulled the letter about Juan from her pocket. "I am very grateful that you're willing to let me tell you about this. A few days ago, I received a letter about my stepson. I have no idea what to do, and Sarah, my daughter, thought you might be able to give me good advice." She unfolded the letter, "It's in Spanish, so…"

"That's all right. Perhaps you just want to show it to me."

He read it carefully, and then handed it back. "Are you concerned that if he tries to contact you, you'll be in danger from the cartel?"

"I just want to find him," Joan said. "I can't imagine the cartel reaches all the way to Ipswich, Massachusetts."

"I think you're probably right about that. I didn't hear talk about it in Boston. But I'll ask around to make sure."

"Thank you, that's very kind. Do you have any thoughts about what he would do if he got to the States? He'll have very little money. He doesn't know English. He's not that physically strong since the civil war in Nicaragua. I mean his strength is coming back, but they almost starved in the mountains. I can't picture how he'll find shelter or food. I wish with all my heart that … ah well. I'm sorry. I'm just plain frightened for him."

"One possibility is that he'll look for farm work. If that happens he might come up this way any time now. Migrant workers tend to travel in groups with a foreman who's bilingual. My job at present is to visit the workers in the farms around here. The name Juan Estrada doesn't ring a bell, but I'll look at my records to be sure."

"Thank you."

"Do you have a photo of him?"

"Yes, I do."

"If you want me to, I'll ask the farmworkers about him. More and more people will be coming soon. I'll keep you informed."

"Thank you so much. That would be wonderful. Perhaps there's something I can do for you some day."

"There's bound to be." With that he stood up, stubbed his cigarette out, put the stub in his pocket and shook her hand again. "Get me that photo and I'll show it around. If I hear anything I'll let you know immediately."

"Thank you again." Joan wanted to hug him, but she knew a strong handshake would have to suffice. She watched as he walked back toward the parking lot, swinging one foot in what looked almost like a dance.

Joan was surprised by how enjoyable it was to be with her family. During the day when everyone was at school or work, she explored the area in her old Karmann Ghia. She hadn't driven a car in years and enjoyed the independence it gave her. She visited the museums in Williamstown and the homes of FDR and Eleanor Roosevelt in Hyde Park, and she walked along the Hudson River, marveling at its beauty. She and Sarah took turns grocery shopping and making supper. She enjoyed trying to please the family with new recipes. Living on her own she'd been making a soup that would last for days. The children took turns helping with the dishes after supper, and that was a good time to be with them one on one and hear how things were going in school and with their friends.

In the evenings she played board games with the children. Kari loved "Clue"; Sam and Joan didn't allow themselves paper and pencil so they were all equally challenged. Chinese Checkers was another favorite, Sam sometimes playing two colored sets of marbles at once.

On her last afternoon in Carleton, Joan took the kids to the Carleton Bookstore to buy them presents. It was her first visit to the bookstore since coming back from Malpaisillo. Richard, the owner, took both her hands in his and said, "How wonderful to see you, Joan. We're so sorry about your husband. Welcome back!"

"Thank you, Richard. It's good to be back."

"Can I find something for you kids?"

"No, thank you," Sam said quickly. "We're going to look around."

"I'm going upstairs to say 'Hi' to Sage," Joan said, "and have one of your famous coffees. I've been looking forward to an espresso for a long time."

At the top of the stairs, Richard's wife, Sage, greeted her with a long hug and then stepping back she said, "We were so sorry to hear about Oscar."

"Thank you." Joan said and willed herself not to cry.

"It's wonderful to see you. Where are you living?"

"Right now I'm living in Ipswich, but," she lowered her voice, as she said something she'd been thinking about, but hadn't yet mentioned to anyone, "I'm considering the possibility of moving closer to here, closer to Sarah and Joe and the kids."

"That's wonderful. Did you hear that we bought the building next door?"

"No, what are you going to do with it?"

"The bookstore is doing so well that Richard wants to expand it to this floor. We'll put the café downstairs next door, where we'll get more walk-ins. We've found a good man to run it."

"You're not going to run it?"

"No, we're making the top floor next door into my studio. It's big and airy and we're putting in sky lights. I've been selling some paintings and we've decided I should paint full time. We'll live on the second-floor next door. Our apartment in this building upstairs will be available in a month or so. Come on up, if you like, I'll show it to you. It's an awful mess, but you won't mind that."

"No, indeed. I'd love to see it."

The apartment was painted white with Sage's brightly-colored abstract paintings on every bit of wall space that wasn't covered by bookcases. The wide-board floors were slightly uneven underfoot. Three floor-to-ceiling windows looked out onto Carleton's Main Street. There were two bedrooms in the back with a bathroom between them. The windows in the back looked out onto the back yards of the stores. The kitchen was in the corner of the living room separated from it by an island with three stools. There was an easel near the corner window with a stool and a table covered with paints and pallets and jars of brushes.

"You've made it so beautiful.," Joan said. "I suppose it's pretty expensive. I mean I imagine you'll get a high rent for it."

"More important than the rent," Sage said firmly, "is to have someone we can count on, someone we feel comfortable with, living here."

"Well, I think it's terrific. Thank you for showing it to me."

As she drove back to Ipswich with Bruce in his carrying case on the floor beside her, the contrast between the fun Joan had had visiting her family and the loneliness she'd experienced in Ipswich, made her wonder what she should do next. Seamus had called to tell her he had taken the photo around to the farms, so far without luck. "But a lot of new workers are coming up from the south in a few months. I'll let you know as soon as I hear anything. Let me know, though, when you come back to visit your family. The new workers may not trust me right away, and a visit from you to the farms telling them about your stepson might be more effective."

When Joan arrived in Ipswich, and let Bruce out of his carrying case, she saw that the fields on either side of the driveway to the mansion glowed in shades of yellow and pale green. The afternoon sun made the long dark shadows of the trees, some with buds, some with tiny leaves, stretch out over the new grass.

She walked slowly up to the mansion and then to the left around the mansion to the path that led through the woods to the Ipswich River. She carefully clambered down the bank and found a mossy boulder near the river to sit on. In the quiet woods with the slow-moving river shining in the sun, she felt that Oscar was very close. She sat very still trying to absorb the feeling of his closeness into her bones so she could carry him with her wherever she went. A stag came down to the opposite shore to drink. He didn't seem aware of Joan sitting across from him until he had drunk his fill and shaken the drops off his head. Then he looked at her. They stared at each other. It could have been three minutes, it could have been twenty. Joan felt surrounded by the present moment.

Chapter Eleven

Maura
Hudson, New York
April 1992

Maura and Seamus talked on the phone every week, but she and the boys stayed at Olivia's apartment while Maura sent applications to twenty-three colleges in New England and bought a second-hand car. Most of the colleges didn't reply to her at all. Those that did said they had no openings. When Seamus told her about an ad for a math teacher in the Hudson High School, Maura decided she had nothing to lose. It would be an added reason to drive to Hudson and have Toby and Ben meet their great uncle and their cousin Caitlin. Olivia had moved back into her apartment, and it was clear that Maura had to get some sort of work, and a place for the three of them to live, as quickly as possible. She called the Hudson High School and made an appointment for the next afternoon.

The beginning of the drive to Hudson was not auspicious. Despite knowing that she needed to go west on Route 90, Maura found herself going east toward the airport and unable to change directions until the airport exit. Then she got lost and drove drearily along the curving roads that surrounded the airport, looking for the way back to Rte. 90. Ben and Toby were arguing in the back seat, and Maura was becoming confused, and worried that she'd be late for her appointment. She pulled off the road at an intersession to read the street signs and look for a hint of how to head west.

There was a man standing at the intersection as cars whizzed by. He was dark-skinned, tall and thin. He carried a paper bag with a sock overflowing the top. He was holding out his thumb, but the cars were going by so fast that it was clearly in vain. Maura had hitch-hiked in England during her college vacations. She'd promised herself then that she would give rides to hitch-hikers when she had a car. But it was different now that she had children in the car with her. She looked at him carefully. Her instinct told her he was both desperate and harmless. She rolled down her window. "Do you need a ride?" He didn't seem to understand the question. She tried again, this time using the Spanish she thought she remembered from high school.

He stared at her. Toby rolled down his window and the children stared back at him. Then he sighed, and said in Spanish, "Yes, please." He opened the passenger door and smiled shyly at the boys in the back seat. They didn't move until Ben held out his hand. The man took Ben's small hand in his for a moment before getting into the passenger seat.

"Where are you going?" Maura asked in ungrammatical Spanish. The man looked dazed. After a moment of silence, she asked, using a combination of gestures and words, "Do you want me to find a policeman to help you?"

The man sat up taller and reached for the door handle. "No police!" he said emphatically.

Maura turned towards him to look into his eyes. She saw gentleness and vulnerability. She looked at her watch and said with more gestures and a few words in both languages, "I'm going to Hudson, New York, three hours to the west. Where are you going?"

"I go Hudson," the man responded quickly.

She decided she didn't have time to figure out what to do with this man until after her job interview. Her uncle would be able to understand what the man really needed. She drove quickly, eager to arrive in time. Ben and Toby now whispered their games or their arguments, she couldn't tell which. Once they were safely back on Rte. 90 going west, she looked at the man beside her. He was asleep.

Three and a half hours later, she parked in the lot of the Hudson High School. All three of her passengers were asleep. "We're here, kids," she said as she unbuckled them. "Please come in with me and wait quietly in the front hall. Toby, I'm going to ask you to look after Ben while I talk with someone in another room. First we'll find a bathroom and get washed up." At the sound of her voice the man stretched and got out of the car. He went with them into the school.

Once the bathrooms were located, Toby and Ben followed the man into one, while Maura used the other. With the sleep washed away from their faces, the four approached the door to the receptionist's office. The lady behind the desk took one look at them and said to Maura's passenger, in a combination of Spanish and English, "Go down those stairs and through the door marked maintenance." Maura wanted to explain but didn't know what to say. The man nodded, let go of Ben's hand, and headed toward the stairs.

A few minutes later the Principal strode into the receptionist's office. He wore a dark grey suit with the jacket unbuttoned to make room for his paunch. He looked surprised and not happy to see the boys. "Keep a good eye on them, will you Martha?" he said to the receptionist. "You kids sit tight; your mom will be back soon," he said to Toby who pulled Ben back when he stood up with Maura. "Come with me," the principal said to Maura, as he turned his back and headed down the hall.

"Where are you from?" he asked as soon as they sat down. "I don't recall seeing you around here."

"At present, I'm staying in Cambridge."

"Cambridge, Mass.? Well, that's a posh academic city. What are you doing there?"

"I've recently returned from England. I was teaching at a university there."

"Oh, a professor, are you? What were you teaching?"

"Philosophy."

"Philosophy! What's that good for?"

"Well, I ..."

"No, don't tell me. I know all I need to know about philosophy. So, what are you doing here? What is a philosophy professor, from England no less, doing in Hudson applying for a job teaching mathematics to high school kids? With all due respect, I'm assuming you got into some sort of difficulties at your last job."

"No, I left the university in good standing. I've come back to the States for personal reasons."

"Oh, I see. Do you have a graduate degree in Mathematics?"

"No, but," she paused for a moment looking for the right words, "I'm comfortable with math. And I'm a good teacher. I taught high school while I was getting my masters..."

"You taught math in the high school?"

"No, it was history, but..."

"I see. Well I'm afraid I'm wasting your time, or vice-versa. We need an accomplished mathematician with teaching experience. We may not be an English university, but we don't let someone who only feels comfortable in a subject teach it to our students." He stood up. "Good luck to you. Can you find your way out?"

"I can. I've had years of teaching experience, and I was hoping that...

"I'm sure. If we decide to teach philosophy, you'll be the first to know."

"Thank you," she said pretending to enjoy his joke as she left the office.

In the receptionist's office the boys were sucking lollipops. Maura looked at the receptionist who shrugged with a smile. "Thank you very much for looking after them," she said. "Let's go kids. We're off to see Uncle Seamus."

"But we have to wait for John!" Toby said.

"John?"

"Our friend in the car!"

Maura realized that Toby was right. She couldn't just leave the man here without making sure he was okay. She turned back to the receptionist, "Has the man we came in with returned from downstairs?"

"No, not yet."

"Toby, did you tell John we would wait for him?"

"No, but…"

"You're right. But let's wait outside. I need some air. If the man comes back, would you tell him we're waiting outside?"

"Sure," said the receptionist, with a wink at Toby.

Outside they sat on the stone steps. "Did John tell you anything about himself?"

"No, Silly, he doesn't talk English."

Maura was silent after this reasonable rebuke. Uncle Seamus will know how to help him, she told herself — a man who doesn't speak English and carries his possessions in a paper bag. At that moment he appeared. Toby jumped up. "We waited for you. I told Mummy to wait for you."

The man beamed at Toby, and then said to Maura, "Thank you. I home now." He reached into Maura's car and took the bag of his possessions out of the passenger seat. Then he shook hands with all three of them, and, fluttering a piece of paper, he walked quickly away, turned a corner and was out of sight. Maura wanted to run after him to find out what had happened, but she had a child holding on to each hand and couldn't.

Chapter Twelve

Joan
Carleton, New York
April 1992

When Joan decided to sell her cottage in Ipswich to rent the apartment over the bookstore, she felt she needed to tell Caleb of her decision. Caleb had been married to Joan's sister, Marianne until her death from cancer five years before. Joan had lived with Caleb and Marianne for the last years of Marianne's life helping to take care of her sister. After Marianne's death, Caleb gave Joan their cottage in Ipswich saying, "I don't have words to thank you for your help, but we want you to have the cottage as a symbol of our gratitude."

When Joan left for Nicaragua she and Caleb had lost touch with each other. He had gone back to work with Doctors Without Borders, traveling round the world as a cardiac surgeon. She addressed her letter to his house in Venice, outside of Los Angeles, but had no idea if or when he would receive it.

> *Dear Caleb,*
>
> *I hope you are well and safe wherever you are. I've come back from Nicaragua where I married Oscar who has died along with two of his children in the war against the Contras. Thus, I have joined you in the experience of widowhood. I find it very much like being forced against my will through a brick wall. On the other side of the wall I see no path at all, just thorny bushes. Is that how it was or still is for you?*
>
> *When peace was declared in Nicaragua, I moved back to the cottage in Ipswich so that Oscar's son could start a business in his dad's house. I am extremely grateful for the wonderful refuge the cottage has afforded me.*
>
> *But I find now that loneliness has overtaken the shock of widowhood, and I am planning to rent an apartment in Carleton to be near Sarah and her family. To do this, I need to sell the cottage.*
>
> *I hope, Caleb, that you'll understand my combination of gratitude for your gift of the cottage and my feeling of wanting, perhaps needing is a better word, to be near my family at this time.*
>
> *All my love, Joanie*

Caleb wrote back express mail.

> *"Dearest Joanie,*
>
> *Of course I understand about loneliness! I'm grateful my kids are all happy in their lives, but I sure wish they lived closer.*

Marianne wanted you to have the cottage as a symbolic thank you for your invaluable help the last years of her life. She wanted to give you something that would make you happy. I'm sure that selling the cottage to live near Sarah would be exactly what she would want you to do.

Is there room in your new apartment for me to come visit? I still haven't met Sarah's husband and their kids. You know, of course, that you are always welcome here.

I'm working at a hospital in downtown L.A. I miss Doctors Without Borders, but I'm getting too old for all that traveling. I'd love to see you – your place or mine, as Mae West would say.

Meanwhile let's stay in close touch.

love, Caleb

Once settled over the Carleton Bookstore, Joan knew she'd made the right decision. She loved being near the family. Bruce seemed to enjoy lying on a windowsill that looked down onto Main Street and watching the people and traffic below him. Joe and Sarah's apartment-warming present was an upright piano. Joan and Kari started taking piano lessons together and could soon play simple duets with Sam accompanying them with his drums.

Soon after Joan arrived, Seamus came for breakfast to give her the map he'd made of the farms in the area. "If you visit the farms and show the workers Juan's photograph and tell them about him, it might help them remember having seen him." Joan had fifty copies made of the photograph and pasted them onto three by five cards. On the other side of the cards she wrote in Spanish, "If you see this man, please ask him to call me…" with her name and phone number.

At first when Joan visited the farms, she avoided the owners and went straight to the trailers the way Seamus did. But on the third day an owner confronted her for trespassing. Unlike Seamus who represented an organization that the farm owners knew of, Joan had no excuse, and from then on she went first to the main farm house or barn and asked to speak to the owner. Some of the owners were willing to look at the photograph. None of them wanted her to speak to their workers directly. Her luck changed when she visited Hillside Orchards. Seamus had warned her about the dogs at Hillside. "They bark a lot but I've never heard of anyone getting bitten."

Sure enough five large dogs greeted her car with ferocious barking and growls when she drove up to the barn. After taking a deep breath, she slowly got out of the car and walked carefully among the dogs to the small door in the side barn marked "Office." The dogs followed her to the door and waited while she knocked. She heard someone say, "Come in." When she opened the door, the dogs almost knocked her over as they crowded through it with her. Inside a woman was kneeling on the floor surrounded by three puppies and their mother. The five dogs who had come in with Joan stopped just inside the door as the woman got to her feet. She looked to be in her forties. She was wearing bluejeans and a sweat shirt. Her blond hair was disheveled around her face.

She looked at Joan and smiled, before saying, "I'm Pam Winfield. Can I help you?"

"Yes, please. My name is Joan Estrada. My stepson has recently come to the states from Nicaragua. He has not been able to get hold of me because I've moved, and I'm wondering if he might be among your workers. His name is Juan Estrada."

"No, I'm sorry. He's not working here."

"Would it be okay if I showed a picture of him to some of your workers to see if they've seen him?"

"Let's see the picture."

Joan handed her one of the cards.

After a moment of looking it over, Pam said, "Everyone comes to the barn at eight in the morning for assignments. If you're here at eight sharp, I'll give you three minutes to explain the situation and give out your cards. Will that be helpful?"

"Very helpful. Thank you so much." They shook hands and Joan headed back out to the car, followed by all five dogs.

The workers the next day were sympathetic and gracious. They all took a card and promised to be in touch if they heard anything. After giving out the assignments for the day, Pam invited Joan into her office for a cup of coffee.

"What sort of work do you do?"

"I'm retired. I was a kindergarten teacher."

"Why are you fluent in Spanish?"

"My husband, Juan's father, was from Nicaragua."

"Can you read and write in Spanish as well?"

"With the help of a dictionary I can."

"Do you know how to type?"

Joan didn't answer, thinking she must have misheard.

"The reason I ask," Pam went on, "is that I could do with help in this office especially from someone who's bilingual."

"Yes, I can type."

"It's a busy time just now, with many new workers arriving next month. You'd meet them all and you'd be corresponding in Spanish with people in the south looking for work. You'd also be in touch with the other farms in the area. We talk back and forth about the workers who are coming because they give other farms as references."

Joan had a strong feeling that Oscar was encouraging her to take this job because working here might be the best way to find Juan, so she said, "When would you like me to start?"

Chapter Thirteen

Maura
Hudson, New York
May 1992

Seamus met Maura and the boys at the parking lot of the Hudson train station. Maura saw that he'd lost weight and his hair was white, but his smile, his wonderful everything-is-going-to-be-okay smile, hadn't changed at all. The boys had never met him, but every Christmas and Easter and on their birthdays they'd received boxes of presents from Aunt Rose and Uncle Seamus, so once out of the car, they ran into his arms to hug him.

When he looked at Maura, his eyes were teary, and as he hugged her he whispered into her ear, "They look so much like your dad." Then he held Maura at arms' length and said, "You, my dear, are beautiful. What happened to that scrawny kid who took off for England against our wishes?" Maura laughed, and they headed up hill, Seamus carrying her backpack over one shoulder and holding Ben's hand. Toby ran ahead of them, showing off his ability to run uphill.

After a couple of blocks they stopped at a Chinese take-out restaurant. This was an entirely new experience for the boys, but above the counter were photographs of the different dishes so the boys chose from them. When Maura was young, her aunt and uncle often celebrated happy events with Chinese take-out. She got a little teary missing her Aunt Rose.

Seamus's apartment was the wide-open attic of a Victorian house. The late afternoon sun poured in through the skylights. The four of them soon dug into the food which the boys decided they loved. They told Seamus about John, and they all wondered aloud about the paper he was fluttering, and where had he disappeared to. After supper they played card games, and then Seamus taught the boys some card tricks that they looked forward to showing off to the next person willing to watch.

Seamus had pushed his bed against the wall with the idea that Maura could sleep there with the boys and nobody would fall off. "I'll sleep on the sofa," he said when Maura protested, "No problem." Once the boys were asleep, he asked Maura, "Do you want to tell me about Terrance?"

Maura didn't know what to say. "I called him and left a message to say we were staying with Olivia. He never responded. The boys don't ask me about him, so we don't talk about it."

"Would you consider taking him back when he comes to

his senses? Could you think of this Carlotta business as a sort of temporary illness?"

"I don't know, Uncle Seamus. But right now I need to focus on getting a job and a place to live." Then Maura told him about the debacle at the high school. When Maura woke up the next morning, she saw that Ben was sleeping on the couch with Seamus. They went out to a diner for breakfast, another first for the boys. "Your great aunt Rose was always the cook in our family," Seamus explained.

"She was a wonderful cook," Maura said as she put out her hand to touch his arm.

"Yes, she was," he said gruffly. "Alright men," he said to the boys, "Let's go find your cousin Caitlin. We're going back in time to Shakespeare's Globe Theater. Let's see if we can find it." The boys jumped up as though it were an Easter egg hunt, and Seamus drove them to Carleton.

Maura had moved in with Uncle Seamus, Aunt Rose and their daughter, Caitlin, when her father, a policeman like Uncle Seamus, was killed while trying to protect people during a shoot-out. Caitlin had been the apple of her parents' eyes and suddenly she had to share the limelight with Maura. They were teenagers at the time and fought and made up and fought again many times. Caitlin was all smiles now, with curly red hair and laughing eyes. She wore jeans and a green tee shirt that proclaimed "Peace." After giving Maura a big hug, she lifted Ben up and together they twirled in a circle to his delight. When Toby raised up his arms, Caitlin took hold of both his hands and swung him around, as everyone stepped out of the way. As Caitlin hugged her father, Maura turned to shake hands with the other person in the room. She was taller than Caitlin and stood as erect as a Degas ballerina. She was dark-skinned and wore a dress of red and yellow stripes, with a narrow cloth of the same material covering her hair.

"My name is Malika," she told Maura. "I'm glad to know you. Cait has told me that you and she were like sisters after your father died."

"Malika is a playwright from Kenya," Caitlin announced. "We're producing one of her plays this summer." Then after a celebratory smile at Malika, she continued, "We're on our own for lunch today. We're between plays and people have dispersed a bit."

For lunch they had a Kenyan specialty called *githeri* that Malika had made from beans and corn. Caitlin had also made macaroni and cheese "in case the boys don't want to try new things." The boys enjoyed the combination of *githeri* and mac and cheese, and Malika was pleased when they asked for seconds of the *githeri*.

After lunch Caitlin and Malika took them on a tour back stage at the theater. The boys tried on hats and fought all over the stage with wooden knives whose blades slid into their handles. When the boys were worn out and panting, Seamus said it was time to leave. After hugs all around, they got back in the car. When Toby asked where they were going, Seamus told him, "Into the woods."

They drove along miles of dirt roads that wound through woods and fields and ended up at "Treehouse Books," a second-hand bookstore, in a refurbished barn, connected by a well-worn path to a farmhouse. Seamus told them he had discovered it while looking for farmworkers' trailers. He'd gone back many times since then, and had become friends with its owner, Maggie. They both had grandparents from Dublin where Maggie had lived as a young child. Maggie's father was from Calcutta, and she'd spent her teenage years there. Seamus, who'd never left the States, told them, "Her stories about Ireland and India make me feel like a traveled man."

Maggie greeted them warmly. She was shorter than Maura, with a round face and red hair that was threaded with grey. She wore a green and blue sari over a yellow blouse. Seamus took Toby and Ben upstairs to what had been the barn's hay loft and now housed the children's books. The three of them settled into an over-sized bean bag chair with "Curious George," "The Adventures of Babar," and "Eloise at the Plaza."

Maggie gave Maura a tour of the store. "This is amazing," Maura said more than once. "You've got books I've looked for in academic libraries and was unable to find."

Maggie smiled and said, "I'm glad you like it. It's involved many years of collecting and selling and collecting again. I've been very lucky with some estate sales of houses with fine libraries. Come on into my kitchen for a minute. I want to make some hot chocolate for the boys and some tea for us."

As she put together a tray of hot chocolate and cookies for the boys, and tea and Irish soda bread and butter for the grownups, she said "My two kids and three grandchildren are living in India. I would like to have long visits with them. Seamus tells me you're a philosophy professor with some sort of personal dilemma. If you would consider remaining here through the next two summers, I'd like to offer you the position of manager of the bookstore so I could travel. Before you decide," she went on quickly, "I want to show you where you and the boys would live."

She showed Maura an apartment on the second floor. There were three rooms, a bathroom and a tiny kitchen with a miniature refrigerator and a hot plate. "Of course, you'd use my kitchen," she said. "Don't decide right now," she went on. "There's not much money involved. I would give you fifty percent of the profit you take in while I'm away, and twenty-five percent when we're both here, which wouldn't be often. The bookstore profits are uncertain, but you'd have no living expenses besides food."

"I don't understand," Maura said, after a moment of wondering if she'd heard her correctly. "You know nothing about me."

"You're wrong there. Seamus is very proud of you. I know you worked your way through college and graduate school after your Dad died. I know you're a college professor." After a minute she added, "I wouldn't dream of offering you this job, but Seamus said that you'd come back to the States too late in the year to find a college position, that you're writing a book, and you have your boys to support. I figure you could spend the time here working on your book and looking for a good position to begin a year from September."

Maura thought of all the applications she'd sent out to no avail. She thought of how good it would be for Toby to go to kindergarten. She thought of how grateful Olivia would be to have her apartment to herself again. She thought of how much she'd already dipped into her savings. She took a deep breath and said, "I think that's a wonderful offer. If you're sure, the boys and I thank you very much. When would you like me to start?"

"As soon as you like. Once you're ready to take over, I'm off to India."

As Seamus drove them back to Hudson, Maura told them about the job. Seamus beamed with pleasure, "What a joy it will be to have you all close."

"From what Maggie said, it sounds as though this was your doing."

"Not at all," he said with a smile.

Chapter Fourteen

Joan
Carleton, New York
May 1992

Joan found she enjoyed the ebb and flow of her work at Hillside Orchards. She liked welcoming the new workers as they arrived. She showed them around their trailers and told the women about the day-care centers and the local schools. She told them about the local grocery store and said that she or Pam would be driving a van there once a week to take workers who didn't have their own transportation. Joan happily chatted in Spanish reveling in the language of Oscar and his family. She gave each family a card with Juan's picture. Everyone was respectful and a little somber as they received it. Some families explained that they too had relatives who had disappeared while crossing the border.

Caleb surprised Joan one evening by calling from New

York City. "I'm at a conference. I thought I'd have to go back to California on Friday, but I have a few days respite. I would love to see you. It's been far too long. Could you come to the city for the weekend?"

"This weekend?"

"Yes, I would have called you earlier, but I just heard from the hospital that my replacement wants to stay until Monday." After a moment he added, "I'm staying at a hotel on West 79th street, and I've already checked that they have a room free for you. Please say you'll come."

"I don't know, Caleb," Joan said, having no idea what a hotel room would cost. "It's sounds great, but I'm only working part time and I'm not sure..."

"Oh, Joanie, I'm sorry I didn't make it clear. You would be my guest: a Broadway play, museums, a stroll across the Brooklyn bridge. You're the New Yorker in the family. Please say you'll come and show me around."

"That sounds wonderful, Caleb; I'd love to do that."

"Good, I'll make the arrangements."

The Lucern in New York City was an old-fashioned hotel, gracious and welcoming. After supper on Friday, Caleb and Joan walked down Broadway to Times Square. They wandered from theater to theater to choose what they would see and to buy tickets for the next night; they settled on *The Crucible*.

On Saturday morning they walked across Central Park

and then continued south and east to the United Nations where they took part in a tour. "I came here when I was young," Joan told Caleb, "In those days anyone, even school girls, could sit in the visitor's gallery while the meetings were happening. Each seat in the visitors' gallery had a phone so we could dial into the translators' booths and have a concurrent translation of what was being said in different languages. I listened in French because that's what I was studying in school. I didn't understand much, but I felt wonderfully cosmopolitan."

When they left the UN, Caleb said, "I think this afternoon is too beautiful to spend in a museum. How about a trip on the Staten Island ferry?"

Standing in the stern, watching the wake of the ferry as the Manhattan skyline became smaller, Joan felt that Oscar was with them in the waves of the wake. The feeling expanded to include Oscar's daughters, Yeni and Eloina, and her own daughter, Angelica. She felt that their lives had become part of the abundance of the sea itself.

That evening at *The Crucible*, Joan cried as she watched people's lives being destroyed by wily teenagers' histrionics. "It's really about McCarthyism," Caleb whispered into her ear when he saw her tears.

Joan was still crying as they began their walk uptown towards the hotel. But when her tears stopped flowing, she realized that her tears had loosened a bit the knot she was carrying in her fears about Juan.

Sunday morning, they walked south through the park but stayed outside of the zoo. Joan had always both hated and loved the zoo as a child. She was eager to see the animals, but felt so sorry for them in their cages that she could barely look at them. The only exception were the seals who seemed to be having fun in their rocky swimming pool. They seemed to enjoy catching the fish thrown to them during feeding time while a large audience clapped and laughed.

They left the park at the fountain on 57th street and walked down Fifth Avenue to Saint Patrick's Cathedral. There Joan took Caleb to see the painting of the Virgin of Guadalupe. "She's the one I pray to when things get rough," she told him.

Caleb then found a statue of St. Luke, "And here's the physician I try to learn from."

When they left the Cathedral, they realized they were going to be late for Caleb's bus to the airport. They began to run, holding hands and laughing as they pulled each other along. At the bus stop on forty-second street, Caleb gave Joan a quick hug before boarding his bus for the airport. Joan walked across the street to Grand Central Station to wait for her train north.

Chapter Fifteen

Hudson, New York
Seamus
June 1992

One morning Seamus took a young farmworker who had a high fever to the Urgent Care Clinic. When the receptionist asked his age, the boy said he was fourteen, but when Seamus had registered him, his green card had said sixteen. Seamus figured the fever must have confused the boy and said so to the receptionist. "Perhaps," she answered, "But those green cards often don't have the right information. They often say what the workers think we want to hear."

Seamus realized he'd never been curious about where or how the workers obtained the green cards that enabled them to apply for jobs and to register for Migrant Advocacy. That afternoon, when he registered a new farmworker, he asked, "Where do you apply for these cards?"

"We can't apply," the young woman said. "We have to

buy them. There's a place near the city."

Seamus almost asked for the details, where outside of the city, how much do they cost, etc. But reminding himself that he was no longer a policeman, he refrained from comment while he completed the registration process. He then drove to the office to tell Jasmine what he had learned.

"Don't tell me about bought cards!" she almost shouted at him. That's none of my business, or yours either! Your job is to write down the number, not to ask where the card comes from. We're here to help people, not to investigate them. You've never worked in the fields. You've never gone hungry to feed your children. You know nothing about it." Jasmine stared at Seamus for a minute, and then added, "If you don't like this work, I suggest you move on."

As Seamus considered how to respond, Jasmine went on in a calmer but disdainful voice, "The problem is that you see these people from a distance. You share a language with them but nothing else. As your supervisor, I feel worried about the workers feeling judged by you, a white policeman."

"Are you firing me because I used to be a policeman?"

"I'm not firing you; it's Jorge Gomez who does that. But I'm putting you on notice that I don't think you're doing the job well. What's more important," she added after a moment, "is that I'm not sure you have it in you to do the job well." After a pause she continued, "I'm talking about your inability to really care about people who are different from yourself."

Seamus wanted to say, "Lady, you know nothing about

it," but instead he grabbed his hat and said, "I'll see you tomorrow if I still have a job." As he walked back to his apartment he wondered if anything Jasmine had said about him was true? He imagined Rose walking beside him and asked her what she thought. The answer he heard was, "You've always cared about the law. That has been your life's work and it's understandable. But perhaps she has a point about understanding people who are different. What about your last visit with Caitlin?"

Seamus had been to visit Caitlin the week before and they hadn't spoken since. Caitlin had invited him for supper, and when he arrived she said, "Malika's rehearsal is running late, so it will be just the two of us." He was glad to have her to himself for a change, and during supper they had an enjoyable time reminiscing about their vacation trips to Maine when Caitlin was a child.

Malika rushed in while they were the doing the dishes together, "I can't find my copy of Act III!"

"It's on the nightstand, on your side of the bed."

"Thank you with all my heart," Malika said, running into the bedroom, and coming out carrying some papers. "It's nice to see you, Mr. Carroll," she said to Seamus as she left. "Your daughter is a life saver!"

After the front door closed, Seamus asked, "You don't have enough beds?"

"Please, Dad, let's not go there."

Seamus said nothing for a moment, considering changing

the subject but not feeling quite able to.

Caitlin spoke into the silence, "We're in love, Dad, just like you and Mom..."

"But the Church..."

"The Church is wrong about this. I don't know what else to say."

Seamus didn't know either, so he gave her a kiss on the cheek, told her he loved her, gathered up his coat and hat, and left.

Now, thinking over what Jasmine had said, and what he thought or perhaps imagined he'd heard from Rose, Seamus called Father Brennan, his old friend as well as his priest, in Boston, and told him about the bought green cards. "Seamus, they have no other way of getting jobs here. They risk their lives to come here so they can support their families back home. You're doing God's work helping them Seamus. I'm sure Rose is looking down on you with gladness in her heart."

Then he called Caitlin. She sounded very glad that they were talking about something new. "Oh Dad, I think Father Brennan's right. What you're doing for these people is important! Remember when I read "Antigone" in high school, and you explained to me about 'a higher law?' Surely feeding their families is more important than having the right kind of papers!"

"There's nothing like hearing one's own words used to argue a different way of looking at things. Thank you,

Sweetheart, and I'm sorry about…"

"Let's not go there, Dad. Not now."

"You're right dear, not now, and thank you again."

Chapter Sixteen

Maura
Treehouse Books
June 1992

Once Maura and the boys were settled in Treehouse Books, Maura wrote Terrance to tell him of their whereabouts. She thought it was important that he and the boys stay in touch and she included some of their art work in a large envelope.

Dear Terrance,

The boys are doing well, although of course they miss you a lot. Toby is in Kindergarten. He's already excelling in numbers and letters. Ben spends the mornings in a nursery school run by a neighbor, and the afternoons with me at the second-hand bookstore where I'm working.

It's on a dirt road quite far from town, but booksellers from New York City and Boston come to buy books and sell them in the cities for double the price. The boys have made friends with a family at a farm nearby, and in the late afternoons we three walk down there to watch the cows being milked.

I'm enclosing, a finger painting by Ben, and a crayon drawing by Toby. The red shape is our bookstore and the grey shape next to it is where we live. In front of the house is Tinkerbell, a barn kitten we've adopted.

I've told the boys that I'm sending their pictures to you. They send you their love as well.

Sincerely, Maura

Terrance wrote her back quickly:

Dear Maura,

I'm so glad things worked out well for you and the boys. I can just picture people from New York and Boston traveling all the way to your little store on a dirt road in the middle of nowhere and being thrilled to find you there, and to pick out the best sellers for the city.

Being separated from you and the boys has been the most difficult thing I've ever done for the sake of my career, of 'our career' as you used to call it. You know better than anyone else the sacrifices that I've made, that you and I have both made, to get my career off the ground. So, I believe that despite everything you of all people will understand why I had to connect myself with Carlotta. There have already been three magazine articles with photographs about our romance. My agent is extremely pleased. He thinks there's a lead role for me in a West End play that's about to be cast.

I hope you'll be happy for me, Maura. I truly believe that if our roles were reversed, I'd be happy for you. Also, I'm hoping that someday our boys will be proud of me as my reputation grows.

Mother is still furious with me. She adamantly refuses to allow me to bring Carlotta into her house — nor will she come to mine if Carlotta is there. All she wants to talk about is how much she's missing the boys and you! Of course she never really understood how important my career was to both of us in the old days.

Perhaps you could write her and try to explain.

Although I love hearing your news and about the boys, your letter has made Carlotta unhappy. She doesn't like to think of my 'past.' Despite being so famous, Carlotta is a little fragile emotionally, so I think it's best if you don't write to me again.

Love always, to you and the boys,

Terrance/Daddy

The combination of having a place to live, and a job seemed to thaw Maura's shock and pain about Terrance's betrayal. She had needed to be numb while she concentrated on survival for herself and the boys. Now Maura found the numbness wearing away, and the pain of being betrayed and abandoned growing, and at times almost overwhelming her. Maggie had left for India two weeks after Maura and the boys had moved in. Her first weeks with Maggie and then on her own had been an exciting learning curve — there was a great deal of information to absorb.

But as soon as Maura felt comfortable in her new job she found she missed teaching. She continued to send applications to colleges and universities, expanding her territory to the entire country, and asking to be considered for a position a year from September. Few colleges acknowledged her letter. Some wrote back to say they no longer had a philosophy department. Maura wondered not only what would happen to her, but to the world itself, if philosophy was no longer being studied. She longed to discuss this with her ex-colleagues in London, but she had the disquieting feeling that they might have been aware of Terrance's affair with Carlotta before she was, and she felt both embarrassed and angry that none of them had told her about it. On the other hand, by not writing to her colleagues, Maura felt she was cutting herself off from a life she'd enjoyed immensely and believed in fervently— discovering, with her colleagues, how to change the world for the better by uncovering and teaching a newly creative way of thinking.

Her consolation was that in the mornings when the bookstore wasn't busy, and Toby and Ben were at school, she could focus on writing her book. It was a comparison of Thoreau's experiences at Walden Pond, where he was searching for the essence of existence by simplifying his life dramatically, and James Baldwin's experiences in Paris, where, for the first time in his life, the color of his skin did not influence how he was perceived.

Maura liked to think of herself as in some ways sharing their experiences. Her life at Treehouse Books was much simpler than the life she had led as an academic in the bustling city of London. Also, at the university she had been respected because of her profession. Now, working in a bookstore there was no reason for strangers to respect her. In this way she felt she was sharing Baldwin's experiences but in reverse.

Chapter Seventeen

Seamus
Hudson, New York
June 1992

Seamus wasn't sure of the law, but he thought that by helping farmworkers that he knew were using fake documents he himself might be committing a crime. That was why, he reasoned, that Jasmine had told him to never tell her about "bought green cards."

Everything got worse one afternoon in June. Seamus was driving Magdalena, a pregnant farmworker home from a job interview, when she said, "Could you stay and have supper with us? Urbelino and I would like to talk with you about something." She was mumbling this in Spanish as though she almost hoped he wouldn't understand her.

"Thank you," he said, "I'd enjoy that very much."

Urbelino welcomed him warmly, gave him a beer and then served them a combination of rice and stewed meat. When Urbelino joined them at the table he said in rather formal Spanish and somewhat gravely, "We are grateful that you are willing to hear what we would like to propose."

Seamus stared at him, but Urbelino's smile softened the formality of his words. Seamus said, "Of course I'm willing to hear what you propose, but I have no idea what it is."

"Magdalena didn't tell you about it?"

"I thought you could explain it better," she said looking down at her lap.

"Well then, I will try. Señor Seamus, you have been very helpful to our family and we are grateful. We have a very difficult dilemma and we would like to tell you about it. Is that agreeable to you?"

"Yes, of course."

"We have a three-year old son. His name is Carlos. He has been living for the last year with my mother-in-law in Mexico. A year ago, when Magdalena came north, she wanted to bring Carlos with her, but the coyote doubled the price for a toddler who might cry when they were hiding. I was in the hospital at the time with a collapsed lung, so Magdalena left Carlos with her mother and came alone." He paused for a minute and reached out his hand to gently touch Magdalena's cheek. Seamus saw that Magdalena was quietly crying.

"All has been well with Carlos and my mother-in-law, Maria, until now. Maria's sister, who lives with them has fallen very ill. She needs to be cared for both night and day. Maria is not able to care for both her sister and Carlos, so she has asked Magdalena to return to Mexico to care for Carlos."

"If I go back now," Magdalena said through her tears, "I don't see how we'll ever afford for me and Carlos and the baby to come north again. My mother is doing her best, but she says she may have to put Carlos in an orphanage."

"I'm so sorry." Seamus could think of nothing else to say.

After a moment Urbelino continued, "I have an idea; actually, Magdalena and I have thought about this a lot together. We have an idea of how to bring Carlos here, but our idea involves you. Shall I tell you our idea?"

"Yes, of course."

"What we would need to do is find a Mexican family living here with a three-year-old son born in the United States. He would need to have a birth certificate, and a passport with a photograph taken when he was a baby. My idea is that they could write a notarized letter giving you permission, as their child's great grandfather, to bring their son back and forth from Mexico. I think you could travel to Mexico using their papers and bring Carlos back pretending that he is your great-grandson, or perhaps, great-great," he augmented, looking at Seamus more closely.

Urbelino began to eat in earnest. Magdalena continued to stare at her hands in her lap. Seamus wondered if he'd understood correctly what had been said. He went over it in his mind and realized that nothing had been vague. He was being asked to bring a child to the States from Mexico using a fake passport, a fake birth certificate, and a fake notarized letter stating that he was the child's great-great-grandfather.

Seamus's head felt like a battle ground between his belief that laws makes civilization possible, and the friendship and sympathy he felt for this pregnant girl and her hard-working husband who were asking him to break many laws at once.

After a silent minute or two, Magdalena looked at Seamus and said, "If I return to Mexico now, I don't know when I'll be able to see Urbelino again. If he returns to Mexico with me, how will we make enough money to feed the family? But if I don't go back to Mexico, my mother may have to put Carlos in an orphanage. Señor Seamus, we would not dream of asking this of you if there were any other way we could think of to bring Carlos here."

After they finished their meal in silence, Seamus said, "I want to thank you for a delicious dinner. I am not able to say anything about your proposal at this time, but ...."

"But will you consider it?" Magdalena interrupted him.

There was a brief silence before Seamus sighed and said. "I will consider it." Then they shook hands and Seamus escaped into the night air.

Chapter Eighteen

Maura
Treehouse Books
July 1992

Dear Maura,

I just picked up your money order at the American Express office. Thank you. You're doing a great job and I'm very grateful. Don't worry if things get a little slow in the summer. When all the garden designing and planting is done, people will come back to the cool (in all senses of the word) book-store looking for distractions. I suggest you put books on interior decorating and antiques as well as gardening on the 'recently-arrived' table. Summer's a time when a lot of weekenders think of redoing their houses and buying expensive antiques.

I like your idea of expanding the travel section. Also, I think you're right that we should have books in as many languages as possible, as well as bilingual dictionaries.

I'm sending you a first edition of "The Portrait of a Lady." I bought it for a song in a bazaar. I think you might be able to sell it for a symphony. Keep up the good work, but go easy on yourself. The last thing I want is for you to get burned out. Please give my love to your wonderful boys, and thank Toby for his glorious drawing of 'Cow Being Milked.'

Big hugs to the three of you, Maggie

ps: Could you tell your uncle Seamus how much I appreciated his letter. Please tell him that the envelope got smudged and I'm not able to read the return address. Perhaps you could let me know his address next time you write.

Maura put a card table in front of the bench outside the bookstore to use as a summer desk. Sometimes neighbors stopped at her outside desk and introduced themselves. They asked about Maggie and told Maura about themselves. There was a cabinet-maker whose wife kept bees. Maura began to display their jars of honey on her inside desk. There was an elderly potter who worked at her wheel in the corner of a neighbor's barn. Almost everyone in the neighborhood, including Maggie, had her cups and bowls in their kitchens. And there was a Rabbi who commuted to his synagogue in Hudson, while his wife played the organ at the local Methodist church. Besides Maura's neighbors, some of her new customers began to come by regularly to buy or exchange books, or just to talk.

Her most interesting customer arrived the first Saturday in July. He was driving a battered old Pontiac. When he got out of the car, Maura realized he was the same man who had driven with them to Hudson. He wore an ironed shirt and slacks and his shoes were polished. He smiled in surprise as he recognized Maura a minute or two after she recognized him.

"I thank you," he said as he held out his hand. "You help me much. You help me job."

"I'm so glad," Maura said, staring a little, because he was so good looking. "Did you find a good job?"

"Yes, good. I keep everything working."

Maura wasn't sure what he meant, so she repeated vaguely, "I'm so glad." What she knew she was glad about was seeing him again. "I'm not sure I ever told you my name. I'm Maura, and you are... John?"

He seemed unsure for a minute, and then he said, "Please call me Juan."

"How did you find us? I mean, did you come here to thank me?"

"I look books."

"Of course, how foolish of me. We have a few books in Spanish. If you like, I'll show you where they are upstairs."

"Children books. I look children books. I learn English."

"We have a big section of children's books. They're also upstairs. Let me take you up and show you where."

While he was upstairs looking at the books, Maura went back downstairs and almost ran along the path to the house. Toby was showing Ben how to draw with the large crayons he'd been given at school. "Kids, guess who's here!"

"Is it Daddy?" Ben asked

"For an instant Toby looked excited, but then seeing his mother's face he said to his brother, "Don't be silly! You know…"

Maura interrupted him. "It's Juan, the man we drove with to Hudson."

"You mean John," shouted Toby.

"John," echoed Ben, although he looked a little vague.

"He asked us to call him Juan, which means John in Spanish. He's upstairs looking at children's books."

"We'll bring him a drawing." Toby said. "And a finger painting" he added looking at his brother. "Go get one of your finger paintings."

When Juan came back outside to Maura's table in front of the store, Toby and Ben were there with paintings and drawings they'd rolled up and secured with a rubber band. Juan spread each picture out flat, pointed to different shapes and was told by the children, using gestures and sometimes animal sounds, what they represented. When Juan understood the description, he repeated the word in English and then in Spanish. The boys and Juan repeated the words back and forth in Spanish and English amid lots of laughter. Then Juan shook hands with each boy as he said in English, "Thank you much."

He had chosen five children's picture books and a Spanish/English dictionary. As Maura rang them up for him, she said, with lots of gestures and a few words in Spanish, "When you finish with these books, you can bring them back, and I'll give you money to buy new books with."

"I come Saturday."

"We'll look forward to seeing you. I hope you like the books."

A week later he brought the five books back, and announced, "I learn all words these books."

"Good for you!" Maura said. "Are you ready for more books?"

"I ready," he said and headed upstairs.

This time the boys followed him upstairs. "I'll show you some of the best books" Toby assured him.

"I can do three puzzles" Ben boasted.

"With help," Toby corrected.

They were upstairs so long that when they came outside they squinted in the sunlight. "Do you want to see the cows?" Toby asked.

"It may be time to milk," Ben stated hopefully. Maura sighed with pleasure as the three walked toward the neighbor's farm hand in hand.

Juan came the following Saturdays. Each time he brought back books and bought new ones. One day he said to Toby and Ben, "You want I read you this? I know all words."

"Sure," Toby said, "I'll help you." Juan sat on the bench outside the store with Toby and Ben on either side. His accent sometimes made it hard for the boys to know what word he was saying. When that happened Toby made Juan repeat the word again and again with the correct pronunciation. Juan could read English better than Toby, but he was amazingly polite about Toby's corrections. "You help me much. You help me learn the English." Toby loved the praise and worked on his own reading skills with his mother in the evenings. From then on Juan's Saturday visits included reading aloud to the boys.

One Saturday morning Ben suggested, "Let's make lemonade for Juan."

"Good idea." Maura said, "Let's make it for everyone. We have some in the freezer. I'll just...."

"Mummy," Toby interrupted, "We can do it. I know where the big pitcher is. I know you put four cans of cold water in with it."

"You're right. That's all there is to it. Then put it in the refrigerator so it will be nice and cold."

"Duh," Toby said. A bad habit Maura thought, that he'd picked up in kindergarten.

One afternoon, after reading aloud to the boys, Juan walked with them to the farm to look at a new-born calf. Maura watched them go, wishing she could join them. It was wonderful for the boys to have a man they could share adventures with. Otherwise it would be strange, she thought, to be growing up with only a mother who couldn't really understand their way of thinking or the way they wanted to explore the world. She decided then and there to buy a soccer ball in the hopes that Juan would play with them. She was a bookish mother and the boys needed active men in their lives as well.

Juan walked back from the farm by himself. "The boys play with baby cats," he explained. He poured himself a cup of lemonade and joined Maura on the bench in front of the store. Together they looked across the road at a tree-lined field being plowed.

"Where do you come from?" Maura asked, her thoughts still on soccer.

"Nicaragua," he said, as though he were confiding a secret.

"Has your family come with you?"

"The wife of my father is in the States."

"And your father?"

"My father and sisters are dead during fighting. They are in the mountain in Nicaragua."

"The fighting?"

"We fight the Contras who try to ruin Nicaragua. Your government help them."

After a minute Maura said, "I was living in England, so I didn't hear much about it. But I remember now that Americans were angry at President Reagan."

Juan didn't say anything for a few minutes as they stared at the fields and at a woodpecker making a jazzy racket. Finally, Maura said, "Is that why you came to the States— because your father and siblings were killed? The fighting is over, isn't it?"

Juan said nothing for a minute, tilting his face up to the sun. Then he said, "Yes, the fighting is over. Maura, you help me much. I tell you story? You no tell?

"Of course."

"I have store sell computers. Mexican from drug cartel grab computer, no pay. I hit him. Before he leave, he say, 'You no hit no person again.'

"Mayor say, 'Here is visa. Here is money. You leave now. Cartel no find you.'"

"Do you think the cartel is still looking for you?"

"I not know. I not look for wife of my father so she be safe from cartel. You tell nobody?"

"Nobody."

Chapter Nineteen

Seamus
Hudson, New York
July 1992

Seamus told Jasmine that he needed to take some time off for personal reasons.

"You don't have vacation time coming for months," she said sternly.

"Yes, I know but I need to do something now. It shouldn't take long. I can work over time when I get back to make up for it."

"I'll give you two weeks unpaid leave. I don't want you trying to work over time while you're dealing with an urgent personal problem."

"Thank you very much." Seamus considered telling her what it was about, but that would involve saying that Magdalena and Urbelino were using fake papers, and Jasmine had told him specifically not to tell her about that. So

Seamus decided to let her believe that someone in his family needed help right away.

He thought about telling Caitlin where he was going. Caitlin would be glad to hear that he was trying to help the family, but she might worry about his safety and beg him to think of some other way to help them. The person he really wanted to tell was Maggie. She had been sending him long wonderful letters about her travels.

He decided that someone local should know where he was going, in case he got stuck in a Mexican jail. He called Maura and asked if they could get together sometime soon without the boys.

"Of course, Uncle Seamus. If you come here tomorrow, we could meet when I close the store at 5:00. The boys have been invited out for supper tomorrow. There's something special on television and a gang of kids are going to watch it together at the farm house down the road."

"Thank you, Maura. I'll see you at 5:00 then."

He was a little early and restless, wandering back and forth on the road in front of the bookstore while Maura said good bye to her last customers. Finally, he sat on the bench outside the store and Maura joined him there.

"Would you like a beer or a cup of tea?"

Seamus appreciated the way Maura always kept beer in the fridge for him. He knew she never drank it. "A beer would be great."

"Alright, I'm going to have some tea. Do you want to come into the house or do you want to talk out here?"

"Let's go in your kitchen so you can make yourself a cup of tea."

When Seamus had his beer and Maura her tea, they settled onto the sofa and Maura said, "Please tell me what's happening."

He told her everything about Urbelino's plan and added, "and now they've found a family willing to help them."

There was a long pause before Maura asked, "Are you considering doing this?"

"Yes, I am."

"Why? I would have thought doing things against the law would be especially hard for you."

"You're right," he told her. "It is." After a deep breath he continued, "but Magdalena and Urbelino are my friends. The money they earn helps support their extended families in Mexico. That's why they need to stay in the States. If I don't do this, a child will be put in an orphanage instead of living with his parents. I've decided that if I can prevent that from happening, inaction on my part would be almost criminal."

"Uncle Seamus, " Maura said, looking worried, "isn't our government cracking down on people who help illegals? Aren't our soldiers shooting people as they cross over? Where would you be coming across the border?"

"Maura dear, I'd be flying. If Mexico lets me and Carlos out of the country, there would be no problems until I landed in the States."

"Why would you have trouble getting him out of Mexico?"

"They might arrest me for trying to kidnap a child. But Magdalena says her mother will be right beside me, and if there is any problem, she'll simply take Carlos back with her. I'll have a copy of the birth certificate of the American child, as well as a notarized letter from his parents saying I can take him to and from Mexico."

"What would your problem be when you land in the States?"

"If they realize that it's a different child, I don't know what they would do, perhaps send us back to Mexico, or arrest me. I don't know. But the point is," he continued after a sigh, "if I do nothing, if I play it safe, this little boy might grow up in an orphanage, or grow up without ever knowing his father!"

Maura was silent for a minute or two. Seamus got up and walked over to a window to look out. "Well, Uncle Seamus," Maura said to his back, "I'm impressed by your courage." After a moment, she added, "And of course, if you get into difficulties, I'll do everything I can to help you, no matter what the law says."

Chapter Twenty

Joan
Carleton, New York
August 1992

Hillside Orchards was very busy. Joan worked full time which she was glad about because Kari and Sam were at sleep-away camps, Sarah was working long hours at the Globe, and Joe was in Italy. The Academy had asked Joe to go to Florence to arrange a trip for the high school chorus for next winter, as well as to interview some would-be exchange students.

Joan enjoyed meeting the farm workers who were coming to harvest the apples. When she showed them the cards with Juan's picture, they looked at her with sympathy. Many of them knew someone who had died trying to cross from Mexico into the States. They didn't tell her their stories, but their eyes did.

Then one Friday morning, Caleb knocked on the office door. It seemed to Joan that he was like Californian sunshine itself. After giving him a big hug, she introduced him to Pam.

He explained that he'd been bumped off a flight from Boston to Los Angeles. "I figured that meant I should rent a car and come visit my sister-in-law."

"I think that means, Joan, that you should take the day off to show Caleb your stomping grounds. I'll see you on Monday." Pam said it in such a way that there was no arguing to be done. Joan simply thanked her, as did Caleb, and they were off.

"Let's drive both cars back to my place," Joan suggested, "and then we can decide what sights you want to see."

"You are the sight I want to see, Joanie." After a long look at her, he continued, "That's a good idea, I'll follow you to Carleton and then maybe we can have breakfast."

"Heavens," Joan said, "You drove all that way without breakfast?"

"I didn't want to miss you — find you'd left town for some reason."

"Yet you didn't call?"

"More romantic, or as you would put it, more fun, driving fast over the Mass turnpike to find you."

Joan had nothing interesting to eat in her apartment, so they went to the bookstore cafe next door and she sipped coffee while Caleb had ham and eggs and a bagel.

"What were you doing in Boston?"

"It was a conference on Hospital Administration. I have a decision to make. When I'm seventy-five I'll retire from cardiac surgery. Either I can leave the hospital all together or I can go into administration. I have a year to make the decision."

"What are the pros and cons?"

"For which?"

"Administration for example."

"I've been in the medical world since college. My happiest memories are of working with Marianne in Africa — people coming to see us frightened and desperate, and leaving us hopeful and on the road to recovery. I can't imagine what life would be like without being involved in helping people recover."

"Could you specialize in cardiology without doing surgery?"

"That sounds so reasonable, but in fact I wouldn't be top notch at it. A great deal has changed since I branched off into surgery."

"What's against going into administration?"

"Well, there too, I'm not sure I'd be good at it. I've spent decades advocating for changes in how hospitals and clinics are administered. Do I really want to face the music and have no one to blame but myself?"

"If you were to retire altogether, what would you enjoy doing?"

"Ah, there's the rub. Since Marianne's death there's very little besides work that feels really pleasurable. I enjoyed being with you in New York City. For that entire weekend I wasn't thinking of patients back in L.A. You, Joanie, make me feel happy."

"Because we've known each other for ever?"

"Maybe, partly, but I think it's more just the way you are. Tell me about you, Joanie. What's your life like here?"

"Well, I too am enjoying my work. After studying Spanish for so long it's a treat to be able to talk with the workers. But, I'm afraid that I'm becoming discouraged about finding Juan. Each morning I pray that he'll appear or call. Each evening I pray that he's safe somewhere. So far none of the workers have seen him in their travels."

"I can imagine that's terribly hard." After a moment he continued, "So, Joanie, I've got twenty-four hours. Can we explore your new neighborhood?"

"Would you like to walk to a waterfall, visit Eleanor Roosevelt's Val Kill, or take a tour boat on the Hudson?"

"All three if possible."

"We'd better get going then," Joan said. He drank the last drop of his coffee and put down enough money for a big tip, and they headed off in Joan's car to Bash Bish Falls.

The path through the woods leading to the falls ran beside a fast-moving wide stream that swirled around boulders, and then the path began to climb a hill so that the stream could no longer be seen but could still be heard. "I feel as though I'm inside a Cézanne painting," Caleb said as they breathed a little more shallowly because of the climb.

"Me too," Joan said, surprised. "Maybe it's because we

grew up in cities and nature was found in museums."

Caleb took her hand as they reached the top of the hill and could hear and then see the roar of the waterfall. They continued to hold hands as they stared in wonder at the waterfall's beauty and power.

After a while Caleb broke the silence by giving her a kiss on the cheek and saying, "Let's go see Eleanor's hideaway."

The tour of Val Kill began with a film of Eleanor Roosevelt's life including images of her roughhousing with her children and swimming with her women friends. There was also a photograph of her in a car by herself heading south, despite having been threatened by the KKK.

When the tour group entered Eleanor's house, Joan thought the living room felt like coziness itself. She wanted very much to unsnap the chord that held tourists to one area and make herself comfortable on a couch to listen in on the conversation Eleanor Roosevelt had once had there with Kennedy before he became President.

After the tour they went to a diner in Hyde Park and ate heartily. Then they drove to the city of Hudson and down to the river where they lolled around for half an hour waiting to board the next tour boat. It was late afternoon—it would be the last boat for the day. And, in fact, they were the only tourists on it. The other passenger was a volunteer being trained by the captain to be a tour guide. The two of them talked about baseball while Caleb and Joan stared along the craggy shorelines watching for, and finally seeing, a bald eagle. "That's how I'd like to fly home," Caleb said, "clinging to the neck feathers of that glorious creature."

When the tour boat returned to the dock, they drove back to Carleton as darkness came on. The plan had been for Caleb to head back to Boston for an early morning flight, but Joan told him about the airport in Hartford. "Perhaps you could get a flight out of there instead? It's much closer. You could sleep in the kids' room."

As Caleb made the phone calls to change his flight, Joan made supper, and opened a bottle of wine. After supper they sat on the couch and finished the wine. They talked about Marianne. Caleb wanted to know what Marianne and Joan were like as children. Their mother had been conservative and strict which had made the sisters rebellious and risk-takers. Joan described some of their adventures exploring parts of Boston that their mother had thought of as "beyond the pale." It felt as though Marianne was sitting next to her whispering in her ear things she'd forgotten that would make Caleb laugh. They talked until just before dawn. It was too late to undress and go to bed, so they lay on the sofa head to feet and slept side by side.

When the alarm went off an hour or so later, they just had time for a long hug and a quick kiss before Caleb headed off for Hartford, accompanied by a map Joan had drawn for him. As she heard the downstairs door slam, she missed him so much she could almost cry with the pain of it.

Chapter Twenty-One

Seamus
Mérida, Mexico
August 1992

Everyone in the plane clapped when they landed in Mérida. Seamus wondered if it was so unusual to land safely? He looked around the airport for Maria and Carlos but saw no older woman with a three-year-old boy. After a few moments, an elderly woman on her own approached him and very shyly mumbled in Spanish, "Could you possibly be Señor Carroll?"

"Yes," Seamus answered, "Are you Señora Perez?" As she nodded smiling, he asked, "Where is Carlos?"

"Carlos is ill with a fever. The doctor says he must not travel until the fever has disappeared."

"I'm sorry to hear it. I'll have to find a hotel room somewhere near by then."

He was wondering if a hotel would take a check from his

bank when Señora Perez said, "We would be honored if you would stay with us. We have three gentlemen who stay with us, and one of them will sleep with a friend during your visit."

"Well, that's very nice of —"

"Perhaps this is for the best," she continued quickly. "You and Carlos can become friends before you take the trip together. I hope you don't mind, but I have told Carlos that his *abuelito* is coming. I thought if he calls you that from the very first, when the customs agent asks him about you, Carlos will say you're his *abuelito*."

"That's a good idea." Seamus liked the idea of being called grandpa.

"Shall we go?"

"I should call my niece. She is expecting us back soon."

"Yes, of course. We will find you a phone you can use. But we must hurry home just now. I left Carlos with his nine-year old cousin."

"I look forward to meeting him. And I thank you for your hospitality."

"My daughter and I cannot thank you enough for what you are doing."

They took an airport shuttle bus to a fancy hotel; then they walked along the narrow streets overflowing with diesel trucks, motorcycles, and honking cars. The noises echoed back and forth against the walls on either side of the road. The diesel fumes made Seamus's eyes water. He felt as though he was walking inside the Sumner Tunnel in Boston, and he sympathized with the workers on the Big Dig there.

Finally, Señora Perez opened a small door that was set inside a large arched door in a windowless wall. With a welcoming smile, she gestured that Seamus should enter. On the other side of the door was a courtyard with buildings on three sides. The high wall between the courtyard and the street muffled the noise and the fumes. Seamus sighed with relief. They entered the building on the right and climbed two flights of narrow stairs. Seamus was grateful for the bannister. The door to an apartment was open, and he could hear a child asking, "Where's my grandmother?" between bursts of coughs.

"I'm right here, Carlos!" Señora Perez called out, as they entered the apartment. "Thank you, Margo." She picked up Carlos, staggering a little with his weight. "Carlos, this is your Grandfather Seamus Carroll. He will visit with us for a few days while you get well. And then you and he will take a voyage to join your mother and father." She put the boy down and asked Seamus, "What would you like Carlos to call you?"

"Grandpa Seamus," he replied, "and I would like you to call me Seamus as well if that is okay."

"That is definitely okay," she said, smiling. Seamus had used the word 'okay' in English because it had become almost universally understood. "Please call me Maria." She let go of Carlos's hand and he immediately came over to Seamus who leaned over to greet him. Carlos looked into his eyes, smiling, and said, "Welcome, Grandpa Seamus."

"Margo, I want to introduce you to my friend Señor Seamus, and I want to thank you very much for taking care of Carlos."

"You're welcome, Aunt Maria." Then Margo turned to Seamus, and continued in slightly slower more careful Spanish, "It is very nice to meet you, Señor Seamus. I will miss Carlos very much when he leaves, but my Aunt Maria has told me that you are taking him to his parents where he will be happy."

Seamus wasn't sure how to respond. He knew he couldn't say, "Perhaps you can visit him there some day." So, instead he said, "Perhaps you and Carlos can keep in touch with each other. You could send him letters maybe including some drawings, and Carlos could send you drawings and his parents could write to you about him."

"That is a good idea, Señor Seamus," Margo said solemnly.

She looked at Maria, who smiled and said, "That will mean a lot to Carlos, Margo. You have been such a good cousin to him. He will miss you and it will help him to know that you are thinking of him, and for him to hear about your life and to see your drawings."

"I will do that, Aunt Maria. I am grateful for the idea, Señor Seamus. I must go and help my mother now. Good-bye, Carlos, Good-bye Aunt Maria, Good-bye Señor Seamus." She ran out the door and they could hear her running down the steep stairs.

Maria gave Seamus a tour of the apartment. They were standing in the main room which was both kitchen and living room. Its only furniture was a table with six chairs. There were two other rooms. In one there were two beds. Maria's sister, Delfina, was asleep in one. Maria explained to him in a whisper, that she and Carlos shared the other bed. The other room had three cots side by side. These were for José, Antonio, and Tomás, who had recently moved to the city. They shared the apartment and helped with expenses. Tomás, she told Seamus, would be sleeping at a friend's during the nights to make room for Seamus. She showed him where to put his small bag. He was glad he'd brought a change of clothes. Then she took him out of the apartment and down the hall to show him the bathroom which was shared by the occupants of the three apartments on that floor.

Back in the main room she invited him to sit down at the table. She gave him a glass of water and a piece of tortilla and said, "We are grateful that you have come. Delfina and I have enjoyed very much having Carlos live with us. He is a wonderful child. But, Delfina, can no longer leave her bed, and I too am finding that my legs sometimes do not want to hold me up."

What Seamus wanted to say was, "I haven't eaten anything since breakfast. Could you make me a sandwich? I could also do with some strong black tea, with milk and honey," But instead he said, "I'm glad I've come as well. Magdalena asked me to be sure to tell you that the farm where they live is way off the main road. Carlos will be able to play outside with his friends without danger."

"Thank you, Seamus, for reassuring me. If you are willing now, and have finished your little meal, I will show you where you can take Carlos outside this afternoon." She took him to a window and pointed down to the courtyard. "There Carlos can play if you are willing to watch him."

"Of course," Seamus said, eager to leave the claustrophobic apartment with its strong smell of illness. He took Carlos's hand, and holding on to the bannister with the other, they carefully descended the stairs into the courtyard. There was a somewhat rickety chair there as well as a tricycle. Carlos immediately got on the tricycle, and Seamus sat down on the chair hoping whoever it belonged to wouldn't mind. Carlos rode the tricycle round and round the courtyard, making noises that imitated the diesel trucks that they could hear on the other side of the door to the street. In between his truck noises Carlos coughed and wheezed. Seamus wondered if whatever was making Delfina so weak might be contagious.

Late that afternoon three young men came into the courtyard carrying groceries. Carlos introduced Seamus to them, and they all went upstairs. After thanking them for the groceries, Maria made tortillas and a soup that included rice and vegetables and a very small amount of meat. They all sat down at the table together, except for Delfina who stayed in bed. Maria took Delfina a little broth and ate almost nothing herself. Nobody suggested a second helping.

After supper, Tomás took a guitar from under his bed, and everyone began to sing. With encouragement from Maria, Carlos climbed onto Seamus's lap. Delfina joined in from her bed in the other room. Seamus was startled by her beautiful soprano voice, in between fits of hacking coughs. They sang for a long time. Carlos fell asleep on Seamus's lap. Seamus began to understand more of the words and joined in on the choruses. The men passed the guitar back and forth among each other. Antonio was the most gifted, and sometimes they just listened to him play remarkable riffs.

Very early the next morning the men breakfasted on some of the left-over soup, while Maria made tortillas for them to take to their jobs. After the men left, Maria offered Carlos, Delfina, and Seamus a little soup and some left-over pieces of tortillas.

Carlos was still coughing and wheezing, so at Maria's suggestion, Seamus took him back downstairs to play in the courtyard. While Carlos went round and round on the tricycle, Seamus moved the rickety chair against a wall so he could lean his head back. He'd been awake most of the night. There was coughing and snoring from both sleeping rooms. His cot felt like a lumpy feeding trough. He leaned back against the wall, shut his eyes and drifted in and out of a half sleep. He was stiff from traveling, exhausted, and extremely hungry. He'd noticed the night before how everyone from those hard-working young men to Carlos himself ate as little as possible to leave enough for everyone else. He wondered if Carlos could get well enough to fly to the States by staying in an apartment, where the air never moved, cooped up with Delfina, who probably had tuberculosis, and without nourishing food.

That afternoon, after a very frugal lunch of more tortilla pieces and broth Maria lay down with Carlos for a nap. Seamus borrowed a basket from Maria who assumed he was going to buy souvenirs. He'd brought extra money in case of an emergency. The emergency was clear. By sharing their food with him, everyone was starving. Once out in the street, buffeted by noise and fumes, he walked until he found a side street too narrow for trucks. Half way down the street was a man selling fruit from a wagon. Seamus bought some pitahaya, a fruit that he'd discovered in the bodega in Hudson. He kept walking down the narrow street looking for a place where he could buy maize and beans to supplement their supplies, but then he thought that might look like charity. Instead he decided to buy things that might be different from what they usually had, to make it more like a gift.

He found a store that sold nuts and cheeses. Almost all the customers were tourists. He enjoyed hearing the French, and Japanese, but even more he enjoyed being taken as a Mexican and asked questions by the tourists. With fruit, nuts and cheeses filling the basket, he turned down another side street where he found an Italian bakery. "Now you're talking," he said to himself. He bought seven different pastry extravaganzas and headed back to Maria's apartment.

That night when he laid the pastries out on a plate at the end of the meal everyone just stared. Then Carlos asked Maria if he might have one. When she nodded, he chose the closest one, and smiled broadly after the first bite. After that everyone chose one, including Delfina.

When the dishes were done, the singing began. Seamus recognized some of the songs from the night before and sang the words of the refrain. He and Rose had sung in the church choir in Boston. The purpose of the choir, the priest had said, was "to open our hearts to God's presence." Here in this kitchen, the singing opened Seamus's heart to the courage of these people as well as their faith and their ability to celebrate life itself. Tears came to his eyes, as he realized how much Rose would have loved to be there with him. She would have cooked up a feast for everyone. She would be sitting on Delfina's bed right now singing with her the lilting soprano harmony. As he fought back his tears, he heard Rose say, "I am here. I'm with you, always. You just keep forgetting."

As they sang, the men seemed to let go of the stiffness of their overworked and undernourished bodies. And Maria and even Delfina seemed to find their youth again, their voices often in harmony with each other. It seemed to Seamus that they knew how to celebrate with their singing how much they cared about each other, their country, and their traditions. They were celebrating how wonderful life is despite its myriad difficulties. And Seamus hoped that with their example and helped by his memories of Rose, he too could learn how to celebrate life itself despite Rose's death.

His days continued in the same pattern, mornings in the courtyard watching Carlos on his tricycle, and afternoons exploring the city and finding interesting food to bring back. Each morning he planned on calling Maura if he could find a public telephone, but in the afternoon, not seeing a place to phone, he decided it would be better to wait one more day. Perhaps Carlos would be well then and he could tell Maura that they were on their way home.

Chapter Twenty-Two

Maura
Treehouse Books
July 1992

Maura had assumed that Seamus would be bringing Carlos back to the States immediately. To her chagrin she realized she'd never actually asked him about the specifics such as how long she should wait before becoming concerned. He had given her the phone number of a lawyer in Boston. "He can sell my house, if it comes to that, to bail me out of jail either in Mexico or in Miami. But don't call him unless it's an emergency. I can hear him ragging on me, calling me Don Quixote battling the windmills. And please don't call Caitlin unless you have to. I don't want her worrying unless it's necessary."

It had been eight days. Maura kept the lawyer's number in her pocket all day. It was Saturday and Juan came to the bookstore in the afternoon, carrying an armful of books to exchange for new ones. His English was improving rapidly. While she prepared to total up the credit she owed him, Juan took a book from the "recently arrived" shelf and settled himself on the upholstered chair next to her desk to read. It was close to five o'clock. Instead of figuring out how much credit Juan had coming, Maura first checked out the other customers who were leaving. Then, feeling a little foolish, but also feeling that she didn't want to be interrupted, Maura went to the door of the bookstore, put out the sign that said, "We Open Again Tomorrow at Nine," and locked the door from the inside. Juan looked up when she did this, but didn't say anything. She rolled her chair out from behind the desk to be closer to Juan's and said, "My uncle went to Mexico recently. He's helping a farmworker family. I haven't heard from him."

Juan seemed to understand not only the words, but her worry as well.

"How travel?"

"By plane."

"How long it makes?"

"Eight days."

"No crashes of planes here and Mexico this week."

"That's true."

"You know name of family? You know what farm they work?"

Maura tried to remember what Seamus had said. "I think

the farm was called River Bank. I remember thinking of the banks of the Nile. The father was called Urbelino. It seemed a strange name for a person who lived in the country."

"Maybe you call to farm and you ask speak to Urbelino?"

"You've been a huge help. I'll do that right now." Maura wanted to hug him. But as she got up to look for the phone number of the farm, she realized that she often wanted to hug Juan. He made her feel less fearful about life itself, and hopeful about the boys having a good life despite being stuck without a father. They hadn't had conversations about any of this. It was just his presence.

She found the phone number for River Bank Farm and called. The woman who answered said that yes, there was a worker there named Urbelino, but that his wife who packed apples had already left the barn for the day. She asked if Maura would like her to give the couple her name and phone number. "We have a policy of not giving out our workers' phone numbers, but I'd be happy to call them and tell them you called."

"Thank you. They won't know my name, but if you could say that I'm Seamus Carroll's niece, I would appreciate it."

"Sorry, I've no idea how to say that in Spanish. All I can do is give them a name and telephone number."

"Okay, my name is Maura, Maura Carroll." And then she gave her number. She hoped that by pretending to be a Carroll she could alert them that she was connected to Seamus.

Juan looked at Maura expectantly when she hung up, "There is a man there named Urbelino. He may be calling back in a few minutes. Would you consider waiting a few more minutes? The problem is he doesn't speak English."

"I wait," Juan said. "What you want I say?"

"Could you ask them if they know Seamus Carroll? If they do, could you tell them that I am his niece and that I'm concerned because I haven't heard from him and I expected him home from Mérida a week ago? Could you ask if there is a phone number where I can reach him in Mérida?" Maura looked carefully to make sure Juan was understanding everything she'd said.

"I ask questions. I tell to you answers. Then I ask more questions."

"Yes, there may be more questions if this is the family that sent my uncle to Mérida. Thank you so much for doing this."

"It is pleasure."

Juan continued to read the book he'd chosen, looking up words in the Spanish English pocket dictionary that he always had with him. The phone rang once but it was Toby asking if he and Ben could spend the night at their friends' house. "There's going to be a movie on TV that we can watch. Please, Mum! It's Snow White!"

Maura spoke then to the friend's dad who said, "Your kids are real peace makers for our rascals. It's a pleasure for us to have them overnight."

"Are you sure?"

"Absolutely! I'll deliver them home tomorrow on our way to church."

"That sounds great. Thank you."

The second time the phone rang it was someone speaking in rapid Spanish. Maura reached the phone toward Juan who quickly got up and took it from her.

She handed him paper and pencil and watched his face closely hoping to understand what he was hearing and saying as they continued in very rapid Spanish. They spoke for a few minutes and then Juan hung the phone up although Maura attempted to stop him so she could ask questions. "Señor Urbelino say he no answer questions," Juan said gently. He say, 'Tell her that Señor Seamus is very good man. He arrive home tonight.' Señor Urbelino will find him at Albany Airport. When I say to him, 'Please wait for questions,' Señor Urbelino says, 'she ask her uncle questions in the morning.' And then he say 'goodbye' and hang up phone."

"Did he say what airline? Or when they would arrive?"

"He say he no answer questions," Juan reminded her.

"I'm so grateful you were here," Maura said after a minute. "I can't thank you enough."

"Maura, you bring me here safe. I thank you for ever and ever."

And then they hugged, a long hug that was not only mutual gratitude but the possibility of more. As they drew back, Maura hoped Juan would kiss her, but Juan said gently, "I go now." He unlocked the door quickly and let himself out.

She heard the engine of his old car sputter and catch, and then she heard the gravel fly as he headed off.

Chapter Twenty-Three

Seamus
The Trip North
August 1992

Seamus knew that Carlos didn't realize that he was about to leave his grandmother and get on a plane with a man he'd only known for a few days. The three of them walked to the nearest hotel that was serviced by an airport shuttle bus. They got on the bus, holding their heads high, knowing they didn't look like tourists. They didn't have to pretend. The bus driver gave Maria a wink and said "Welcome little man" to Carlos.

They arrived at the airport too late for Seamus to call Maura. Maria promised she would call Magdalena to tell her when they were arriving. Maria held Carlos's hand while Seamus bought their tickets. There was a long line behind them, many passengers exclaiming loudly that if they couldn't buy their tickets soon they would miss their flight.

The young girl behind the counter was flustered and asked no questions when Seamus handed her the fake passport for Carlos.

As they walked toward the security gate, Carlos walked between them holding onto a hand of each. At the security gate Maria lifted Carlos up, kissed him and said, "Have a good trip with your grandfather and tell your mom and dad how much I love them and miss them." She then handed Carlos into Seamus's arms and stepped back, not wanting to emphasize to the guard how much darker her skin was than Seamus's.

The guard, a man, who looked to Seamus to be too old to be forced to stand on his feet all day, took the two passports and asked, "Who's the guardian?"

"His parents are in New York," Seamus said, reaching for the letter from the couple of the other child. Seamus kept his focus on Carlos, while the guard read the letter. He hoped that Carlos would look away so there'd be less of him to see when the guard compared him to the photo in the passport. But Carlos seemed to be fascinated by the guard and beamed at him as though they were old friends.

The guard stamped the passports and handed them and the letter to Seamus, but his eyes were on Carlos. "Have a good trip, my young friend" he said, as he ushered them toward the security gate where someone would go through Seamus's back pack that was now heavier with Carlos' clothes and a few toys.

Seamus turned to give Maria a wave, but Maria was walking away wiping her eyes. Seamus thought Carlos might cry when he realized that Maria was no longer with them, but Carlos continued to stare at the guard, looking back over Seamus's shoulder, as Seamus carried him, stumbling a little under the weight, toward the waiting area.

It wasn't until they boarded the plane and were in their seats that Carlos asked about Maria. "She can't come with us on this trip," Seamus said, trying to tell the truth but not to frighten him. "We're on our way to see your mom and dad. Do you remember them?"

Carlos said, "Yes," and then almost immediately fell fast asleep as though the emotions of the day had exhausted him. Seamus buckled him in, and prayed for a smooth transition at Kennedy airport where they would change for a plane to Albany.

When they arrived at Kennedy, there were long lines waiting to go through customs. Seamus joined the line for US Citizens. He was carrying Carlos who drowsed against his shoulder. His back pack hung heavy on the other shoulder. A guard beckoned to Seamus. Could they already tell that something was wrong? But then the guard inserted Seamus in the front of a long line, explaining to the young couple that he'd put him in front of, "We need to give these guys a break. Otherwise that little one is going to wake up and start to wail, and we'll all be in trouble." The custom's official seemed to feel the same. He unzipped the back pack glanced inside and then stamped both the passports Seamus handed him. Carlos had gotten them through.

Carlos woke up on the plane to Albany and ate the pretzels and peanuts that had been passed out. Seamus walked him up the aisle to the bathroom which was much too small for a man and a toddler, but Carlos found it fascinating. When they deplaned in Albany, Carlos recognized his mother immediately. Seamus let go of his hand as Carlos ran toward her. Magdalena was too pregnant to bend down to pick him up, but Urbelino did. He caught Carlos in his arms and lifted him up, so he could hug and kiss them both at once. Then Magdalena, with tears in her eyes, gave Seamus a hug. Urbelino handed Carlos over to Magdalena and gave Seamus a strong handshake, and Seamus handed him a plastic bag of toys and clothes, as well as somebody else's passport, birth certificate, and a letter that didn't tell the truth.

Chapter Twenty-Four

Joan
August 1992
Carleton, New York

Joan was very grateful to Seamus for all he was doing to help her find Juan. When he called to say, "One of the farmworker families has invited me to a party. They said I could bring a friend. Would you like to go?"

Joan said, "Thank you, I'd like that a lot."

The party was in a trailer at the end of an unkempt dirt road riddled with potholes. Seamus parked next to trucks and cars that all looked to Joan as though they'd had quite a past. There were eight or nine children of various ages chasing a large beach ball around the trailer, the older children carefully avoided running into the toddlers. A boy, who looked to Joan to be about three years old, broke off from the group for a minute to throw his arms around Seamus's legs. Then without a word he went back to the game.

A card table was set up outside the trailer; it was covered with paper plates, plastic forks and spoons, and a very large pot of tamales. There was a cooler on the ground beside the table overflowing with beer and soda. A group of men were talking and laughing as they drank and watched the children. One of the men came toward them and greeted Seamus with a handshake and then a friendly slap on his back. Seamus introduced Joan, but she didn't catch his name. After a friendly nod and smile at Joan, the man gestured toward the trailer, and then took Seamus over to his friends and every one of the men shook hands with him. Joan did what she realized was expected of her and headed for the stairs up to the door of the trailer. Before she got to the stairs, the door opened and a very pregnant woman bearing a large platter of meat, came carefully down them. She placed the platter on the table and then turned to Seamus and greeted him as an old friend. Seamus introduced Joan to her, and Magdalena then introduced Joan to the women who had followed her down the stairs. Everyone, Joan noticed, seemed very glad to see Seamus, and their pleasure at his being there overflowed into gracious smiles at her as well.

As people were beginning to be served, there was a clap of thunder, and rain began to pour down. The men gathered the table and the cooler, the women picked up the platter and the pot of tamales. The older children gathered the toddlers, and everyone went inside. The trailer was as crowded, Joan thought, as a New York subway car in rush hour, but everyone's plate somehow got filled with meat and tamales. Men and women stood talking and laughing in groups shoulder to shoulder while the children pushed between and among them, the smallest ones being lifted high in people's arms. Joan was part of a group of women talking about the difficulties of losing weight after giving birth. She loved to be chatting in Spanish. All would be perfect, she thought, if only Juan could be standing nearby, perhaps telling the men about computers.

When Seamus drove her back to Carleton that night, the rain had stopped. Clouds moved quickly hiding and exposing the stars and the moon intermittently. They talked about the party and how much Joan enjoyed his friends. "It was wonderful, in a way, being the only North Americans there," she said. "It was almost as though I was back in Nicaragua."

"Any news from the Mayor's office?"

"None at all. His secretary promised to write me as soon as she heard anything. To tell you the truth, sometimes I think Juan has died and is with his father and sisters." After a few minutes Joan spoke again into the darkness. "I don't think I've told you about my daughter, Angelica."

"No, I didn't know Sarah had a sister. But the name, Angelica, sounds familiar."

"She was a painter. She lived for a while in Boston and had a show at a gallery on Newbury Street. She was schizophrenic. She'd been in and out of hospitals since she was a teenager, and five years ago she could bear the illness no longer and took her own life."

After a few moments of silence, Seamus said, "I saw that show. Rose and I went together. That's where I heard the name Angelica. That's how she signed her paintings. I was astounded by them. Rose realized first how special they were. She told me to stand still in front of a painting that looked almost entirely black. If you looked long enough slowly other colors showed themselves through the blackness. Rose said it was looking into somebody's soul." After they were both silent for a few minutes, Seamus asked, "How were you able to bear it when she ... when she took her own life?"

Joan sighed deeply before admitting, "At first I didn't know if I could go on living — having been such a failure as a mother. It took months of despair before I allowed myself to realize that I had done everything I could to make her well. Neither I nor her doctors had been able to help her. That's when I decided to go to Nicaragua with Witness for Peace."

"And that's where you met Oscar."

"Yes."

"Isn't it strange that such a tragedy would lead to your marrying Oscar!"

"Yes, life is very strange."

"Before we adopted Caitlin, Rose had a miscarriage. She went into a terrible spiral of depression and we were warned not to try to conceive again. Six months later Caitlin's birth mother was killed during a shoot-out. Caitlin was only a few weeks old and nobody could be found willing to claim kinship with her. I told Rose about the baby, and we began the paper work involved in adopting her. I think Caitlin may have saved Rose's life. Everything changed as soon as she became our daughter. My wonderful Rose became her old self and more…." Seamus seemed to interrupt himself as he thought about Rose. But after a few moments he went on, "My Caitlin is in love with a woman. Does that seem like illness to you?"

"No, Seamus, it doesn't. I think we're born with different preferences."

"I feel as though she's leaving me as she travels down that path."

"Leaving you in what way?"

"She's turning her back on her mother and me by insisting on doing something that the Church says is sinful."

"Is that what your priest says?"

"The whippersnapper priest in Hudson mumbles so there's no telling what he's saying. It's the church that says it." After a long silence, Seamus said, "Rose once told me that she asked Father Brennan about it. He's our priest back in Boston. She was surprised and almost angry at what he said."

After a minute or two, Joan asked, "What did Father Brennan say?"

"He said, 'I hope Caitlin finds a man or a woman to love the way you and Seamus love each other.' I'd forgotten all about that."

Seamus was silent as they drove on. When Joan thanked him and got out of the car in Carleton, Seamus mumbled, "You're welcome." But it was clear that his thoughts were elsewhere.

Chapter Twenty-Five

Maura
Treehouse Books
September 1992

The trees were turning every possible color and Maura felt dreamily as though she were living inside a glorious painting. A letter from Terrance, the first since he'd asked her not to write to him, startled her awake. She waited to read it until the boys were asleep. Then with a glass of wine and the letter in one hand, she gathered Tinkerbell up from a comfortable chair, settled herself in it with Tinkerbell on her lap, took a few sips of wine and slit open the envelope.

Dearest Maura,

We said that our love for each other would last forever. As parents we counted on each other's help to give our sons the best life possible.

I can't explain how I forgot all this briefly. All I can say is that my career was going downhill, and I thought that being

*seen with a famous model would send it rising again. And
you, darling Maura, who helped me so much, you know how
hard I've tried to make this challenging career work, for both
of us.*

*Carlotta is completely over. She's working in Paris now. I've
got a few auditions coming up. Maybe I'll get lucky. But
much more important is that I'm hoping and praying that
you and the boys will come home* toute suite.

Please forgive me, my beloved Maura!

> *Your old flame, and husband, Terrance*

Maura sat very still, remembering Terrance as a fellow
student in college, blond and handsome. They'd married the
day after graduation. Terrance got a job modeling swim suits,
which led to a role in a soap opera. For seven months they
were wealthy beyond their dreams. They paid off their college
loans and Maura began graduate school. When Terrance's
character in the soap opera was murdered, Terrance began
experiencing the ebb and flow of acting jobs, and Maura
began teaching at London University to bring in the stable
salary they needed. They didn't mind the feast and famine
way of life until Toby was born. Terrance then began to work
as a bar tender between jobs, and when Ben arrived, Terrance
tried to get modeling jobs again, but he was no longer
photogenic enough.

Maura knew how much her husband had loved his career.
He'd been a good father and a good husband for years, but
could she forgive his asking her and the boys to move out?

The next afternoon, Seamus visited the bookstore, and looking at Maura askance he said, "You look the way you sometimes did as a teenager when you were missing your Dad."

After a sigh, Maura pulled the letter out of her pocket and handed it to him. He flattened it out, read it twice and then carefully folded it and handed it back. After a moment he said, "I don't know if this is good news or bad. I'd sure miss you and the boys if you were to go back to England. I suppose he can't come here? Become an actor in New York City?

"Uncle Seamus, I don't know if I can forgive him. The truth is, and I'm realizing it as I say it, I don't know if I want to forgive him."

Maura expected her uncle to tell her how important it is for couples to stay together for the sake of their children. He took both her hands in his, as though she were a child again, "You know I love you, and want the best for you. But, Maura, I don't know what would be the best. Ben and Toby seem very happy here, and Maggie tells me you're doing a grand job with the bookstore." After a moment he added, "Whatever you decide to do, I'll have your back."

Maura did not tell Ben and Toby that their father had written. After they were asleep, she went out to the bench in front of the store. The night was cloudless, and she felt that perhaps the light of the almost full moon and the brightness of the stars might help clarify her thinking. It was beginning to occur to her that it might be possible that she could fall out of love with Terrance.

Juan had been laid off from his job as a maintenance man in the school in Hudson for the month of August. His friend with the car had left on a road trip, so Maura and the boys drove into Hudson early each morning to bring Juan to the bookstore before it opened. Juan had found a second-hand computer to fix up and install for the store. In the mornings he worked on setting up the computer with a variety of programs to save Maura time in her research and accounting. In the afternoons he and the boys went for walks bringing back samples of plants and rocks to look up in the natural history books. Sometimes the boys accompanied Juan to the farm when he was asked to help with the harvesting. After supper, often cooked by Juan, Maura and the boys would drive him back to Hudson.

The owner of a house down the road had told his neighbors when he left for vacation that they were welcome to swim in his pond. So, on Mondays and Tuesdays when the bookstore was closed, Maura, Juan and the boys walked down the road with towels, bathing suits and a picnic. Juan quickly taught Ben and Toby how to swim, and the four of them were often giddy with pleasure as they swam, had splashing fights, or dove to find interesting rocks at the bottom of the pond.

Now, sitting on her bench under the stars in a cool clear night of September, Maura tried to imagine how she would have responded to Terrance if his letter had come a month or two earlier. She believed that parents should try to stay together, even when the going gets rough. Also, until Carlotta had come into their lives, Maura had been happy in her marriage.

At least she thought she had. She wondered now if she and the boys had left for America so quickly not only because she was furious about Carlotta, but also because she was realizing that Terrance was no longer the man she'd once believed him to be. Perhaps Carlotta had been an excuse for her, as well as a temptation for Terrance.

The next morning she knew what she wanted to say, and after the school bus picked up the boys, she wrote her reply.

Dear Old Flame,

That may sum things up exactly. I was crazy about you. I assumed we'd stay married forever. I did everything I could to help your career. But you thought I was so unattractive that being married to me was hurting your image. Well so be it. I'm sure there are other Carlottas in the wings. Good luck. Let me know if you're in movies that you want the boys to see.

Go in peace, Maura

Terrance's reply came within the week showing the expensive stamps that had hurried it.

Dearest Maura,

Everything you said is true except that I never thought you were unattractive. What I thought was that I looked a little humdrum being married with kids. I don't know — she just lifted me up and then dumped me in the garbage. It'll never happen again. I've learned my lesson.

I understand that you're angry, but what about the boys? Why don't you bring them home for a visit and we can talk about things? I'm confident that we can find the spark again. You're the most wonderful woman in the world.

I love you, Terrance

ps: I'd send you plane tickets, but I'm a little low on cash just now. I've got an audition on Friday and should be in the pink by the time you get here.

pps: How's your book coming? I'd love to read it. If I get this role, you'll be able to write full time. Always love, Terrance

It was Saturday morning and bookstore customers were beginning to arrive. Maura folded Terrance's letter, put it in her desk drawer, and began to read a copy of Friday's *New York Times* that a customer had left the day before. She looked up as she folded a section of the *Times* and saw through the window the gloriously colorful trees. She could hear customers laughing upstairs. Juan would be arriving soon.

"Look at this, Mum!" Ben called up to her. He and Toby were working on a project on the floor in front of the wood stove. Maura put the newspaper on her desk and stared down at an elaborate castle made of wooden blocks complete with a blue tissue paper moat with a few twig boats sailing round it. Tinkerbell was stretched out beside it looking like a guardian dragon. The boys stared up at her beaming with pride.

"That's beautiful!" she said, at the same time wondering, "Am I doing what's best for them, or am I being selfish?"

Chapter Twenty-Six

Joan
Carleton, New York
October 1992

Towards the end of October Joan said good-bye to the Latino workers, family after family, as they headed south in their over-crowded cars to pick oranges in Florida. With their leaving went the hope that Juan might appear this season looking for work. After the last family had gone, Pam and Joan swept out the trailers, turned off the water, and drained the pipes. As they worked together Pam said, "I'm wondering if you want to continue working through the winter. There's plenty of paperwork year-round, and I find that doing it with you makes it almost fun. What about three days a week?"

"Yes," Joan said, surprising herself because she hadn't thought about it. "I'd like that. Thank you."

"Good. We'll take a break for a couple of weeks just to catch our breath."

When Joan went home she thought about her two-week vacation. She decided that what she wanted to do was visit Caleb. She wanted to walk along the beach that she had explored with Marianne. She wished she'd kept a journal during the last years of Marianne's life. Perhaps being back at Venice Beach would remind her of the intense wonder about life itself that the two of them had experienced as Marianne fought against cancer.

Caleb's response to her call was, "It will be wonderful to have you. You'll make the cottage a real home again."

"We'll miss you, Mom," Sarah said, "but of course the kids will be happy to have Bruce visit us for a while. Please give Uncle Caleb our love."

Caleb gave Joan a long hug at the LAX airport. Then he drove her to Venice and parked on Main Street. He gave her the keys to the cottage which was half way down the Paloma Avenue walkway. "I've got to get back to the hospital. I bought salmon to grill for supper. Is that still one of your favorites?" He took her suitcase out of the back seat, gave her a quick kiss on the cheek and said, "I'm glad you're here," before he got back into the car and drove away.

Once in the familiar cottage, Joan put her suitcase in the upstairs guest bedroom. She made herself a sandwich from the brie and dark German bread she found in the refrigerator, poured herself a glass of wine from an open bottle, and took her plate and glass onto the front porch where she had eaten supper almost every night during the last years of Marianne's life. In the evenings Marianne and Caleb watched television in their bedroom with their supper on trays that Joan prepared.

Joan remembered as she ate how grateful she'd been for those times of silence, knowing that Marianne would not call out asking for something or frightened because of a new pain. When Caleb was home, he took full care of her. Joan was free to walk on the boardwalk or even go to a movie. The evenings had a celebratory quality because of how confined she sometimes felt during the day when she needed to be within earshot of Marianne's needs.

Now, after washing her dishes, Joan went for a walk on the boardwalk heading north toward the Santa Monica Pier. The last day Marianne and she had walked there arm and arm, they'd gotten only a few yards before Marianne was ready to sit down on the low stone wall that separated the beach from the boardwalk. Marianne began to cry silently. Joan held her hand and they cried together, until the boardwalk, and the people walking by, disappeared behind the waterfall of their tears. Three weeks later Joan held Marianne's hand as the end came. Her last words had been, "Look at the light!"

Caleb worked long days at the hospital. Joan tidied the house, took walks, studied his cookbooks and bought groceries to make elaborate dinners each evening. They ate on the back porch, lit with a candelabra that Marianne had brought back from Israel. "This is lovely," Caleb said the first night. "It's romantic. From a novel I mean," he added quickly.

"It is nice." Joan said. "Something we can't do in upstate New York in November."

Joan loved walking on the beach. The seagulls and sandpipers seemed surprisingly comfortable with the people who played volley-ball, built sand castles, and ran races amongst them. The east coast shore birds were less at ease with people, and despite Joan's many walks along the Ipswich beach, she'd never been so close to the birds, and able to see the details of the coloring in their feathers. She began taking Marianne's camera to the beach, after asking Caleb who said, "She would be pleased to know you were using it." She took 'portraits' of the birds watching her as she watched them.

Sometimes she sat on the sand, stared at the waves, and thought about Oscar. She remembered the trip they'd made with his children to the beach. Oscar had surprised her by taking her hand as they floated on their backs in the calm sea. They'd fallen in love through gestures and laughter, and, later, in the way their bodies spoke to each other. She missed hugely the comfort that Oscar's physical presence had given her.

She enjoyed creating meals of different ethnicities for Caleb. He and Marianne had served with Doctors Without Borders all over the world. Over their candle-lit dinners on the porch surrounded by the gentle warm night, Caleb told Joan stories about their experiences in Africa, the Far East, and Latin America.

Joan found herself touching Caleb's arm or his shoulder for no reason at all. He never responded in kind. She became self-conscious about it and told herself to stop, but found herself doing it again. She longed for physical contact. Caleb was an old friend; he was also her brother-in-law. Surely there was nothing wrong in emphasizing a point or expressing her friendship by giving him a pat on the shoulder. But perhaps there was, because Caleb never, after his first hug of welcome, touched her at all.

One evening, as they sat on the porch after dinner Joan said, "Sometimes I feel I may have made a mistake leaving Malpaisillo so quickly. Did it help you, after Marianne died, to leave here and move into an apartment near the hospital? Did that turn out to be a good way of dealing with grief?"

"Yes and no. It meant that I could work longer hours at the hospital – and I owed them lots of hours. But I longed for the beach and came out here whenever I could."

"Did it help not being in touch with me for a while? Remember you told me that you were trying not to relive what had happened and that we shouldn't talk on the phone for a bit?"

"Yes, I remember. That was a suggestion from my grief counselor. Looking back, I see that she was wrong. I wanted to talk with you about Marianne, but the counselor made me believe that by talking about her, I was reveling in the pain rather than healing it. She said I was like a child picking at a scab. Finally I realized she was the wrong counselor. Do you want to talk with me about Oscar?"

"Not now, but thank you for asking. This has been a real vacation. I think being here, where you and Marianne and I were so close as she fought the good fight has been healing for me. I need to leave the day after tomorrow. Sarah called this afternoon. Joe is going to a music teachers' conference in Hawaii and she wants me to take care of the kids so she can go with him."

"Have you ever been to Hawaii?"

"No, have you?"

"Not yet, but, perhaps you and I should go sometime. Doctors sometimes have conferences there as well."

"I look forward to it." Joan had no idea what she was talking about. Why on earth would Caleb want to take her to Hawaii?

The next morning, after Caleb left for work, the phone rang. Joan let the answering machine pick it up until she heard Pam's voice and then she grabbed it. "Did you hear the news?"

"What happened?"

"There was a shootout in León. Twelve leaders of a Mexican drug cartel were killed. I wonder if that includes the man you told me about that's menacing Juan?"

"Wouldn't that be wonderful! I'll call the Mayor's office

right now and let you know."

Maria answered on the first ring. "I've been trying to call you," she said. "Yes, Raul Ozwekas was killed. The police raided during some sort of a leaders' meeting and got them all. Juan has nothing to fear now. If only we can find him to tell him!"

"From your mouth to God's ear," Joan said.

Chapter Twenty-Seven

Seamus
Hudson, New York
October 1992

One Saturday night when heavy rain was turning back and forth into sleet and pelting the windows, Seamus was answering one of Maggie's letters from India. She'd described the colors of people's clothes, the markets, and the prayer flags high up in the barren mountains. Her descriptions of her adventures sometimes made Seamus wonder if he should throw caution to the wind and join her, as she often suggested. She told him about her grandson, Michael, "He's thirteen but seems much younger. He refuses to interact with any of us, won't look directly at us, and sometimes runs into the street as though he wants to cause a crash. My daughter, Hannah, finds him very difficult to handle, as do I."

There was no mention of the boy's father, which made Seamus wonder if Maggie might be bringing her daughter and grandson back to the States. He found himself imagining ways he could be helpful to the little boy, and make things easier for Maggie and her daughter.

His thoughts were interrupted by a call from Jorge Gomez. After announcing his name Jorge Gomez asked, "Is it true what I've heard?"

He sounded to Seamus like a new detective just starting out on his job. The only possible response was, "I don't know what you've heard?"

"Is it true that you kidnapped a child in Mexico to give to a family in the States?"

"I didn't kidnap anybody. I brought a Mexican boy here to live with his parents at their request and at the request of his grandmother in Mexico."

"Did Immigration know what you were doing?"

"No."

"Then you broke both federal and local laws."

"Perhaps, but his parents..."

"There's no perhaps about it! Listen Mr. Carroll, I'm sure you thought you had a good reason. I don't need to hear what it was. You broke the law while working for an organization that is funded by federal grants. We could lose our funding if this gets out."

"I wasn't..."

"I know. You did it on your own time. That makes no difference. You are, or rather you were, a representative of Migrant Advocacy. Your employment is terminated as of today."

Seamus's response, sounded foolish to his own ears even as he said it. "Thank you, Sir."

It must have sounded odd to Mr. Gomez as well, for he said, "You're welcome." and hung up.

Half an hour later Seamus's supervisor, Jasmine, called. "I just got off the phone with Jorge Gomez. It sounded as though he was describing a nightmare he'd had with you as the bogey man. He said he'd already called you. Can you tell me what it's about?"

Seamus told her the story, and added, "I hope I haven't made difficulties for you. It didn't occur to me that what I was doing could harm Migrant Advocacy."

"Don't you worry about that! I don't think Jorge could have understood what you were doing. I've known him for years. I'm going to call him tomorrow. Come in on Monday and let's talk."

"I've already been fired."

"I'll talk with him tomorrow. Please come in on Monday."

"Alright, I'll see you then."

On Monday morning, it was Jasmine who brought the coffee and donuts. Seamus had forgotten all about them. Jasmine seemed to have guessed as much and carried on the tradition herself. "First of all," Jasmine said between bites, "I want you to know that we're in the same boat."

"What do you mean?"

"I've known Jorge Gomez for five years. I assumed I could talk some sense into him. I figured he hadn't gotten the story straight and that once he understood what had actually happened he would want to make much of you instead of firing you."

"What did he say?"

"He said that he had no choice, that his job was to keep Migrant Advocacy afloat, and that if it became known that you had broken the law while employed by Migrant Advocacy, the funding from the federal government would dry up immediately. He said he could lose his job if he let you stay.

Seamus took a sip of hot coffee before he said, "Of course I meant no harm to Migrant Advocacy. I assumed I could do whatever I wanted to on my own time."

"Well, we're in the same boat."

"What boat is that?"

"I've been fired as well."

"You!"

"Well not fired, exactly, but unemployed. I told Jorge that if he was going to let you go, he would lose me as well."

"Why did you say that?"

"Seamus, I thought you were uppity. I thought you patronized the workers. I had no idea that you were willing to risk jail for them. You did something extraordinary. I don't want to be part of an organization that would fire you for doing that."

"But what you do here is important! How will the workers manage without you?"

"Well it's interesting that you should ask me that. I've been thinking of opening my own business."

"What would you do?"

"More or less what I do now. Help people with the paper work they need to access the services available to them. Probably do a lot more outreach. It wouldn't be just for farm workers. There's a large immigrant population in Hudson that I bet don't know about things like WIC and Medicaid."

"But how would…"

"Of course, I would need a partner," Jasmine interrupted him. "Someone who is not only bi-lingual but willing to go out on a limb for people. What do you think?"

Seamus was quiet for a minute, trying to take it all in. Jasmine didn't wait for him to respond but went on, "Of course money is a question. I think everyone would want to pay for help of this kind, but they wouldn't be able to afford much."

"Could you do the paper work in their apartments and trailers?" Seamus asked after a moment.

"Sure."

"So, we wouldn't need to pay for an office." Seamus hadn't meant to say 'we' but he had.

"Right. I feel sure that there's plenty of people who need our help. It might just take a while to find them. Meanwhile," she continued after a moment, "paying my rent might become an issue. Gordon hates his job stocking shelves at Walmart. Maybe he should go back to farm work. He can do everything on a farm—he's worked on all the different equipment. We could live in a farm trailer like the old days."

"You've just given me an idea."

"That's what I've been trying to do."

"My daughter, Caitlin, told me that her maintenance man at the Globe up and quit."

"What's the Globe?"

"It's an acting company in Carleton. Some of the actors and staff, like Caitlin, and the former maintenance man, live on the property. Does Gordon know how to plow?"

"You're talking about a farmer."

"I meant snow."

"How different can it be?"

"Exactly."

"What else does the maintenance man do?"

"What made me think of the job for him was what you said about farm equipment. I think the maintenance man is on call all the time to fix whatever breaks down. That's why he has to live there. Do you think your husband would like that kind of job?"

"I think he'd like it a lot. He can fix farm machinery, so he can probably fix anything else. He used to fix up the trailers that we lived in. He even made some furniture. It sounds right up his alley."

Chapter Twenty-Eight

Maura
Treehouse Books
November 1992

Dearest Maura,

I got the part. I think just being in touch with you gave me good luck. We're in rehearsals but we've got two weeks off at Christmas because the director promised his wife a trip to the Bahamas.

So, I said to myself, "Forget the Bahamas, I want to spend Christmas with my family!!!"

I figure you might need to keep the store open, so I can help you out by chilling with the boys.

On your days off we can go to New York City. There's a play I want to see — I've heard they're considering bringing it here, and I want to see if there's a good role to audition for.

It will be like old times, and I can't wait.

love, Terrance

ps: I got your phone number from Mum, so I'll call you with the flight number. I'll book a connecting plane from New York City to Albany so you won't have so far to drive."

It was Wednesday morning. The store was full of customers looking for inexpensive Christmas presents. Maura realized immediately that she'd made a mistake opening Terrance's letter when there was no time or privacy to think about what he'd said. She quickly shoved the letter into the drawer as the phone rang. She desperately hoped it wasn't Terrance.

It was Caitlin. "Dad wants to do Christmas here. Malika and I will do the cooking. Dad will bring wine, and he suggested I ask you to make a fruitcake. He said it's an English specialty and you pour rum on it and light it on fire."

"That takes months to make, but I'll see if I can find one to buy. So, count on me for desert of one sort or another, but..."

She was about to tell Caitlin about Terrance's letter when Caitlin said, "Listen, Maura, I had the most amazing conversation with Dad just now."

"What do you mean?"

"First off he asked me if Malika was planning to stay in this country. I told him she was. Malika's mother was an American, so she has dual citizenship. Then Dad asked if Malika and I were planning to continue living together. I almost told him to buzz off at that, but luckily I didn't because he went on to say, 'I mean are you a couple? Do you plan to stay together as a couple?' I said, 'Yes, we're just as much a couple as you and Mom were.' I may have sounded a little defiant."

"My guess is that you did."

"And then he said, 'In that case I think your love for each other should be celebrated.' When I asked what he meant, he said, 'I think we should have a celebration with flowers, music, and good food. I think we should ask Father Brennan if he could come and bless your union, and we should invite your friends to witness and celebrate your love for each other.'

"That's what he said! I made him repeat it because I thought I'd misheard. When he said it again, I began to cry, and then so did he. Malika and I are going over there for supper to make plans, figure out a date and all that. But I'm inviting you and the boys right this minute."

"Thank you, we accept with great pleasure." As Maura said that she was hoping that it wouldn't be until after Terrance was back in England. She wanted him to meet as few people as possible. What she really wanted was for him not to come. But she didn't think she could get in the way of his seeing his sons. "Do you have any idea when the wedding will be?"

"You know, of course, that we can't get married."

"What do you plan to call it if not a wedding?"

"We haven't gotten that far. Do you have thoughts?"

"Well it's about commitment…"

"Yes, it is, but that word, commitment, makes me think of prison. And what Malika and I have is the exact opposite of prison."

That evening the phrase 'the exact opposite of prison' rattled around in Maura as she made supper for the boys, washed their backs in their shared bath, sang nursery rhymes with them as they got into pajamas, and then read aloud from *Winnie the Pooh*. As she washed the dishes, no longer being distracted by the boys and their needs, she had to look at the images those words conjured up.

Would it be like a prison to go back to Terrance? Had Terrance felt that he was in prison with her when he took up with Carlotta? What did marriage vows mean — should people stay married even if being together felt like being in prison? Most of all what did it mean for the children when a couple separated? Had she been unwittingly hurting the boys by the three of them becoming such good friends with a man who was not their father? Terrance's letter felt like a bomb that had gone off in her lap. She had mentioned it to nobody. But now she realized she was going to have to tell Juan! She couldn't let him be blindsided by Terrance who would, she felt sure, realize how much she liked Juan, and do everything possible to break off their friendship.

The next Saturday it was in fact Juan who brought the subject up. He was sitting in the chair next to Maura's desk, reading a bilingual book of Latin American poetry, comparing the Spanish and English, and sometimes asking Maura what one of the English words meant. The boys were at the farm. Maura was doing paperwork, feeling extremely grateful to have this gentle, wise, fun-loving man sitting next to her. He looked up, and instead of asking about a word he said, "The father of Toby and Ben, he is not living?"

Maura was startled and then grateful for the question. "No," She said. "He's alive. He lives in England."

"You, Ben, and Toby here as vacation?"

"No," she repeated, "their father and I no longer live together."

"Is it possible that I ask to you why?"

"He fell in love with another woman."

"He marry her?"

"No, after a while she left him."

"Now he live alone?"

"Yes."

"He want you and boys return?"

"Yes. How did you know?"

"You good lady, boys good, he want all together."

"When we were all together, he preferred someone else."

"You return to England?"

Juan seemed to be making this question sound more lighthearted than he felt. "The boys and I will stay here," Maura said, making her decision as she said it.

"The father, he come here to see you and the boys? He come here to ask of you to return with him to England?"

This time Maura didn't ask how he knew. She realized that somehow Juan who couldn't read complicated English could read her like a book. She looked at him in both gratitude and pain, and he looked back showing peaceful understanding as well as his own pain. Finally, she said, "Yes, he wants to come for two weeks for Christmas. I don't want him to come," she added quickly, "but I don't think I can step between him and his children."

"The boys are happy he comes?"

"I haven't told them."

"May I ask to you why?"

"I'm hoping he'll change his mind."

"I go home now." Juan said as he stood up.

"Please don't go." Maura struggled to her feet, her chair too close to the desk. "He's not coming today. He's going to let me know when, so I can pick him up at the airport."

"I think I am wrong to play together with you and with your sons. I think I am wrong no ask about father of sons. I am sorry. I go now." He left quickly leaving his book on the chair, closing the door firmly, revving up the car and making the gravel fly.

Maura felt abandoned. She'd felt the same way when Terrance told her about Carlotta. How could she have let Terrance do this to her twice?

Chapter Twenty-Nine

Seamus
Hudson, New York
November 1992

Seamus and Jasmine picked up Gordon at Walmart and drove to the Globe theater. Seamus had called Caitlin earlier, and she met them outside the theater to give them a tour.

"We don't perform on Monday and Tuesday, but I can introduce you to a couple of the set builders. First, I want to show you the theater." She turned on the lights as they entered the foyer where the tickets were purchased, and then they walked through heavy doors into the theater itself, pitch black until she reached for the lights, and then bright and colorful. "The idea was to copy the Globe Theater in London where Shakespeare's plays were performed. That's why it's in the round and why the stage juts out into the audience."

She took them back stage where they looked into dressing rooms and then outside behind the theater to a large barn-like building where James, a grey-haired African-American, and Tim, a middle-aged Chinese man, were painting a large backdrop of a wide empty highway that became narrower and narrower until it disappeared in the distance. "We're doing *Waiting for Godot* next," Caitlin explained. She introduced Gordon and Jasmine. James said, "I think it's better if we don't shake hands," as he showed his paint-stained one. "Hey, Seamus, good to see you."

"And you, James. I heard your granddaughter got into Vassar."

"She did indeed."

"Congratulations to you both."

"Thank you."

"I'm going to show them the apartment upstairs," Caitlin said, "Do you think it's locked?"

"I know it isn't," Tim said.

"We've just come from sweeping it out and washing the windows like you asked us," James added, with a wink at Gordon. "We made it as presentable as possible."

"Thank you both. Very thoughtful," Caitlin said, and she led Gordon and Jasmine, with Seamus following, to the back of the shed and up a flight of wooden stairs to the second floor. The apartment was one large room the length and width of the entire building. There was a small bathroom in one corner, and next to it the kitchen sink, a stove and refrigerator. In the opposite corner was a small wood stove with a pile of wood beside it. Other than those appliances, there was just space. The floor was made of wide boards and the walls were white-washed. There were three sky lights, that even in cloudy December let in enough light to make the place feel airy. There were two small windows one at either end of the peaked roof. "There's not much of a view, I'm afraid," Caitlin said, "but at least there's lots of light."

Jasmine and Gordon looked at each other and grinned.

As they walked back to the house where Caitlin and Malika lived, Caitlin asked Gordon about his work experiences. "I've been working on people's farms since I was thirteen. I don't know much, or anything really, about plowing snow, but I've plowed just about everything else. I've done a lot of mowing. I've also done some fixing of tractors and mowers. For a couple of years I worked next to a guy whose whole job was fixing machinery. He kind of took me under his wing and taught me a lot."

"Have you done any building with wood?"

"In some of the farms our job was to fix up the old barns. I've done a bit of furniture making as well, just stools and tables. Some farms give us trailers with almost nothing in them, and we have to learn how to make do."

"What about things like stopped-up toilets?"

"Oh yeah, stopped-up toilets, leaky faucets. We're always our own plumbers in the trailers."

Back at the house, Caitlin introduced Jasmine and Gordon to Malika. While Malika served them tea and muffins, Caitlin excused herself. "I'll be back in a few minutes."

When she returned, Caitlin had James and Tim with her. After everyone had more tea and muffins, they sat down, and James and Tim asked questions about technical aspects of what Gordon had done in terms of fixing machinery and refurbishing barns. Then after a quiet nod from both of them, Caitlin said, "Gordon, we'd like to offer you the position of maintenance man for the Globe. You would be in charge of every aspect of maintenance. As a member of the staff you would get a percentage of what the theater takes in. I have to warn you, that sometimes doesn't add up to much. But you would have free housing and health insurance." Without waiting for an answer, Caitlin turned to Jasmine, "Usually when we provide housing, we ask that both adults join our staff. But, since we don't have a position for you at present, and since we need your husband's expertise so urgently, we're making an exception in your case."

Jasmine looked at Gordon who beamed with joy. Gordon had followed her to Hudson leaving the farm work he'd enjoyed and working instead at Walmart, which he detested, so that she could advance her career. Now his expertise was such that she was able to follow him into a new community while continuing to work in whatever way she wanted. "Thank you," was all she could think of to say.

"Yes, thank you," Gordon said, smiling at everyone. "It all sounds wonderful."

Seamus helped Gordon and Jasmine move into their new

apartment at the Globe. Seamus and Jasmine were making plans for their new business at the same time as packing up for the move. Jasmine created a five-by-seven card on the computer that described how they could help people obtain healthcare, education, for their children and themselves, and legal counsel. It had English on one side and Spanish on the other. Together they visited the farms and neighborhoods in Hudson where Latinos and other recent immigrants lived, introducing themselves, handing out their cards, and answering questions.

Since they no longer had an office, Seamus said that if people did not want to discuss their situations in their own homes, they could come to his apartment for privacy. Seamus moved his furniture around so his apartment looked more like an office. It worked out well until a neighbor complained to his landlady who told him he'd have to leave if he continued to bring anyone besides his family or close friends into her house.

That stymied them briefly until Seamus received a letter from Maggie.

Dear Seamus,

Maura tells me of the wonderful work that you're doing. She also told me about your trip to Mérida and how it cost you your job.

Seamus, you let me babble on to you in long letters about my children and my travels, and you keep to yourself your own challenges and adventures! It's not fair! I'm missing you,

Seamus. I miss our long talks at the bookstore. When I think of home, I remember how much I enjoyed your stories about policing the streets of Boston.

Maura and I have a suggestion for you. What about setting up a table and a couple of chairs upstairs in the bookstore right next to the children's section? That way parents could keep an eye on their children while they fill in forms. You could have your own phone up there with an answering machine instead of a secretary. What do you think?

Well, my friend, let me know if this would be helpful. I'd love to be part of the good work that you're doing. And please stay in closer touch with your slightly homesick friend,

Maggie

After talking it over with Jasmine, Seamus wrote Maggie back the same day.

Dear Maggie,

Your generosity will save our business and keep me from becoming homeless. I love your stories. Please keep them coming. If I have another adventure, I'll tell you about it right away.

All I can say about missing, is that I think of you every day.

Seamus

Chapter Thirty

Joan
Carleton, New York
December, 1992

Sarah told Joan that Lark Academy had invited her and the children to accompany Joe and his choir students to Italy over Christmas vacation.

"That's wonderful!" Joan exclaimed, suppressing a qualm at being left alone over Christmas. The next two weeks as the family planned and packed for the trip, Joan sounded even to herself like a Greek Chorus repeating how happy she was for them. Then, she drove them to the Albany airport and waved them off.

She too had vacation time. Hillsdale Orchards was closed until January 6th. She decided to visit Caleb. He'd said in his last letter how much he'd enjoyed their time together and that he looked forward to another visit "'Your place or mine' as Mae West used to say."

But when Joan called Caleb, he said, "Joanie, I'm so sorry.

I'm off to South Africa to see Ethan and William. We planned it months ago."

"Good for you. Please give them big hugs from me."

"I will, thank you. We'll talk soon. Love you."

"Love you too," Joan answered vaguely. She'd spent Christmases alone before, recently in Malpaisillo when Oscar and his children were fighting in the mountains. But without knowing exactly why, she dreaded this Christmas on her own. She felt as though she'd been abandoned by her family, although she knew she should be thrilled that they were enjoying Christmas in Italy.

She went to midnight Mass on Christmas Eve. The church was lit by candles, with reading lights over the lectern and the musicians' stands. There was a grey-haired man with a robust voice who made his guitar sound like his best friend, as though the two of them could do anything together, and a young woman who sang a contralto harmony with him. The beauty of their music brought Joan to tears. After Mass she lit a candle for Juan and knelt by it to pray until the church was almost empty.

Christmas morning was sunny and mild. Joan was almost surprised to see that her apartment looked exactly as it had the week before. Feeling sorry for herself had gotten in the way of buying a wreath, or a tree, and she'd put the few cards she'd received into a drawer instead of displaying them. She'd even forgotten to consider that the stores would be closed on Christmas day, and was surprised, when she wandered into the kitchen, to see how empty the refrigerator was.

After a breakfast of leftover risotto from the night before, she took a walk along the road that led out of Carleton towards the dairy farms. The fields on either side of the road had large patches of melting snow amongst the hay stubble and brambles. She walked for almost an hour taking off her jacket and tying it around her waist.

She thought about Caleb, and about his youngest son, Ethan, who had fallen in love with William at Pratt University where they'd studied architecture. William was from South Africa, and had come to Pratt on a scholarship with the understanding that he would return to his country to build practical and aesthetically pleasing houses for the homeless. Ethan went with him. He had come back to Venice Beach with his two brothers five years before at the end of Marianne's life. Joan remembered how well he had looked, and how happy his stories were about making a difference in the townships around Pretoria.

As she turned back toward Carleton, she sighed with pleasure remembering that all three of Caleb's and Marianne's sons, her nephews, were living with people they loved and doing work they cared about. By the time she got back to town and climbed the stairs to her apartment, she wondered why on earth she'd made such a fuss about the family leaving her over Christmas.

Chapter Thirty-One

Maura
Treehouse Books
January 1993

Christmas came and went. Terrance didn't call or write. Maura was glad she'd told nobody besides Juan about the letter he'd sent. She intensely wished that she hadn't told Juan. She hadn't seen or heard from him since that day.

She and the boys spent Christmas Eve with Seamus. They'd decorated a wreath with origami doves for Seamus's door. When they arrived, he had already set his tree up and decorated it with tiny blue lights. At the foot of the tree on a snowy mountain of white tissue paper was the complicated creche that Maura remembered from her childhood. The boys got down on their knees to look at it and to move sheep and donkeys and wise men into new arrangements, just as Maura and Caitlin had done when they were young. "Where is baby Jesus?" Toby asked.

"I think we'll find him there in the morning," Seamus told

him.

Supper was tiny pizzas made out of English muffins. The boys were in charge of decorating each half muffin with sauce, bits of sausage, peppers, mushrooms, and cheese. Each miniature pizza was critiqued and praised as though it were a colorful sculpture, before it went into the oven, and then again as it was eaten. The boys beamed with pleasure. They spent the night with Seamus and drove with him to Caitlin and Malika's in the morning. The theater was closed for the holidays and almost everyone had gone home to family or friends for Christmas.

Earlier in the week Maura had brought to Caitlin's house two Christmas stockings filled with presents for the boys, as well as presents for under the tree. When they arrived Christmas morning, Maura saw that Caitlin and Malika had added six more stockings — hanging all eight from a shelf near the wood-burning stove. Maura was grateful that neither Toby nor Ben wondered aloud how Santa Clause had arrived since there was no open fire place. She wondered at the number of stockings until there was a knocking at the door and Jasmine and Gordon came in carrying gifts for under the tree. Then after a toast to Christmas, champagne for the adults and apple cider for the boys, everyone cheered and laughed and kissed each other as they opened the stockings from Santa Clause and then the presents from under the tree. Toby's favorite present was an ant farm — white sand with a group of ants captured between two plates of glass so he could watch their comings and goings. Ben's favorite was a large brightly-colored velvety turtle that Malika had made for him because Ben loved the story of the race between the turtle and the hare.

Caitlin had asked the children what they wanted to eat on Christmas day, and she and Malika had followed their desires exactly. They all feasted on macaroni and cheese, carrot sticks, and creamed spinach. For desert Maura had brought an imported fruitcake and some rum to pour over it before lighting it with a match. Watching the rum burn made Maura think of past Christmases in London. The boys too looked a little dazed as they watched. They never asked about Terrance. Maura didn't know if it was because they never thought about him or if they didn't dare ask because they didn't want to know the answer.

Maura and the boys had made Juan a huge Christmas card that included drawings and finger paintings and a love poem by Rubén Darío that Maura had copied out in both languages. They'd sewn the pages together into a booklet and wrapped it with gift paper inside a home-made envelope of large newsprint with Juan's name writ large on both sides. After leaving the Globe, and driving Seamus home, they drove over to Juan's house to deliver the package. They knew which was his building, but they didn't know which was his apartment. In those early summer mornings, he had always been waiting for them on the sidewalk. His name was not beside any of the bells, so they left the large package leaning up against the locked front door and hoped for the best.

In the weeks that followed when Juan didn't come to the bookstore or call to thank them for the card, Maura and the boys discussed whether they should make a new one for him and try again to deliver it. Maura felt almost desperate — not only because of Juan's silence but because she was lying to the boys by not telling them why Juan was staying away. She wasn't ready to talk with them about Terrance, especially now that she didn't know what had become of him.

Finally, a letter arrived.

"Dear Maura,

Well, time sure does fly. I'm sorry I didn't get across the pond over Christmas, but a bunch of us decided to go to Paris for the holiday. And once there, although it certainly was not my intention to see her, I bumped into Carlotta. I guess we're more important to each other than I had realized. Anyway, we've been visiting back and forth and it's possible that Carlotta is a little bit pregnant.

So, as you can see, there's nothing I can do but get divorced, whether I want to or not. My lawyer will be sending you papers to fill out. Luckily for you I'm in the pink financially just now. Otherwise, according to my lawyer, I could ask you to support me, since you did so in the past. But instead I'm enclosing a money order for a hundred pounds. Please buy the boys some bang-up presents from me.

So, dearest Maura, we had a good run. No regrets on my side and I hope not on yours as well. You always were the strong one. I will love and respect you always, and I hope you'll feel the same about me.

With best wishes for a wonderful future, Terrance
ps: Of course I'll want to see the boys when they're bigger
and can travel on their own, but I've told my lawyer that
you're the best mum in the world and you're welcome to have
full custody of them. I knew that would please you.

The letter made Maura feel as though she'd inadvertently gotten onto the Cyclone roller coaster in Coney Island. Her emotions seemed to be whirling too fast to even know what they were. The only emotion she could catch hold of was the desire, it felt more like a need, to see Juan. She called down to the farm and asked her neighbor if she would mind looking after the boys for a few hours after school. "I'd be happy to. Toby is actually helping my Joe learn how to read."

Maura closed the bookstore early, drove into Hudson, and parked in front of Juan's building. About a half an hour later, she saw him walking home, wrapped up in a scarf, and heavy jacket. She got out of the car and ran to meet him. "I really need to talk with you," she said breathlessly, "and to show you something."

Juan smiled at her, held her by both shoulders and said, "My house is your house." They went up two flights and he opened the door to the apartment he shared with his friend. It was small, but well organized as though they were on a boat — everything seemed stowed away in case of a storm. The apartment had two large windows onto the street, and the late afternoon light poured in before the sun began to set.

They sat on the couch and Maura gave Juan Terrance's letter to read. After he read it, she said, "He's not coming, not ever. He's getting divorced from me. Please come back to the bookstore. I miss you so much, and the boys miss you. We miss you terribly!" When Juan didn't say anything, Maura said, "To begin with, please say you'll come with me and the boys to a sort of marriage celebration for my cousin Caitlin and her friend, Malika. It's next Saturday."

After a moment Juan said, "Yes, if you want, I come."

"Wonderful!" Maura said. "The boys and I will pick you up here at 2:00. I'm closing the store for the afternoon."

"I wait for you here."

They stood up together. They stared at each other for a minute. "I see you and the boys next Saturday," he whispered.

Maura was too happy to say anything but "Yes."

Chapter Thirty-Two

Joan
The Globe
February 1993

Joan was surprised by an invitation to "A Celebration of Caitlin Carroll and Malika Mwangi becoming Life Partners on Valentine's Day." That same morning Seamus called, "Did you get the invitation?"

"I did. It came this morning. Congratulations."

"Thank you. You know I wasn't always happy about their friendship."

"I remember that." Joan tried not to sound ironic.

"I was a narrow-minded idiot."

"You were a concerned father. Are you happy about it now?"

"Very happy."

"What made you change your mind?"

"I was in Mexico recently, for... for a sort of short vacation. The people I stayed with were desperately poor and extraordinarily generous! Watching them respond to their poverty in that way shook something free in me. You should have heard their singing! They found their extremely difficult lives worthy of celebration. Since I've been back, that experience has grown in me, like tight buds on a thorny rose bush opening slowly. I realize now what Caitlin has been telling me for months, that her love for Malika is the same as my love for her mother. Such a love needs to be celebrated! I hope you'll come."

"Are you sure your daughter will want me there?"

"Yes, and I want you to meet my niece and her boys."

Valentine's Day was sunny and brisk. Malika and Caitlin's house was overflowing with their friends and family. After Seamus welcomed everyone, he introduced Father Brennan, "One of my oldest friends who has always done what he could, not to keep me on the straight and narrow, but to show me again and again that God loves us, all of us, exactly as we are."

Father Brennan wore a collar but no cassock. Caitlin and Malika wore pale yellow skirts under white tunics embroidered with flowers. The three stood together in the shape of a triangle, their families and friends around them.

Father Brennan said, "We have come here to celebrate Malika and Caitlin and to express our joy in their decision to become life partners.

Then Caitlin held both of Malika's hands as she said,

"Malika, you are my joy, my adventure, my refuge. May God let it be so forever."

Still holding hands, Malika said, "Caitlin, you are the keel of my boat, the lighthouse on a stormy night, the buoys that guide me home. May God let it be so forever."

Father Brennan raised his hands above their heads and said, "May God bless Malika Mwangi and Caitlin Carroll as they travel together for the rest of their lives. May joy rain down upon them as God accompanies them on their journey! Amen."

At the back of the crowd a group of actors from the Globe began to sing "All You Need Is Love" and everyone joined in and laughed and clapped when Caitlin and Malika kissed each other full on the mouth, and then took turns hugging Father Brennan.

As people began to move around, Joan was struck by the sight of the back of a tall thin dark-haired man. She stood stock still for a moment and then she began to push herself toward the front of the crowd, elbowing her way through strangers who stepped back to let her pass.

She didn't say a word until she had passed the man and was able to turn and look at him full on. And then she still didn't speak. Neither did Juan. They stood and stared at each other until Joan was blinded by tears and Juan rushed forward to embrace her.

After the celebration, Seamus, Maura, Juan, Toby and Ben

went back to Joan's apartment. At Caitlin's insistence, they took with them two bottles of champagne and a basket of French bread, brie, imported salamis, and fresh figs. They sat around Joan's living room, nibbling and sipping, and listening to Juan. Ben was fast asleep on Juan's lap, undisturbed by Juan talking rapidly in Spanish. Every once in a while, Juan exchanged smiles with Maura. It was clear to everyone that they shared their own language. Maura didn't care that she couldn't understand what Juan was saying. He would tell her later and meanwhile she basked in his happiness at finding his stepmother.

Seamus asked in Spanish, "But after Maura brought you to the school in Hudson, what did you do next?"

"For some reason the receptionist assumed that I was there to apply for the position of assistant to the maintenance man. She sent me, without asking any questions, not that I could have understood them, down to a workshop in the basement. I felt as though I were in a dream, or a nightmare, so I went."

"That's where my luck changed completely. No, that's not true. My luck had changed when this beautiful woman picked me up from the street and drove me to Hudson. I just didn't know it at the time. But in the workroom, a very friendly Puerto Rican guy took one look at me and began talking in Spanish.

"'What's your experience with maintenance?' was his first question. I was bewildered, but so grateful to be hearing

Spanish, that I mumbled something about projects my dad and I had done fixing up the house in Malpaisillo.

"'Where are you from?' he asked. So I told him.

"'And what the Hell are you doing here?'

"I told him the whole story. I was exhausted and bewildered, and it was such a relief to be speaking in Spanish it all just came out.

"'One of my cousins was killed by the cartel. Come with me,' was his answer. I followed him back upstairs to the receptionist where he asked if we could talk with Mrs. Greyson. Of course, I didn't understand what the two of them were saying at the time, but Fidel explained it later. The receptionist told him that the woman in charge of hiring staff for the building had left for the day and because the need for maintenance staff was an emergency she had given Fidel carte blanche to hire whom he wanted. All she needed was the name, social security number, phone number and home address. Fidel wrote a bunch of stuff down on a piece of paper, introduced me to the receptionist and then took me back downstairs.

"'You're going to stay with me,' he said, 'until you make enough money to find an apartment of your own.' He wrote the social security number he'd made up for me on a piece of paper, and his address. I'll meet you there at five o'clock tonight. Here's a key. It's straight down Warren Street, two blocks over from here. You can't miss it. I'll see you there. Do you need money?'

"I said I didn't. I had exchanged all the money I'd been given before leaving Managua and I had twenty dollars left.

"'Good,' he said, 'hang on to it. Here's another twenty; there's a bodega one block past where we're living. Buy us some food that you're comfortable cooking. Now get out of here. I've got work to do.'

"'Can't I help you now?' I said.

"'No, that would look peculiar. I don't want anyone asking questions. You'll start on Monday.'"

Juan looked around, first at Maura and then at Joan, and smiled broadly. "I've been there ever since. I can't wait to introduce him to you, Juana."

"Were you looking for me all this time?"

"No, I was warned not to, in order to protect you from the cartel."

"I have good news for you."

"It can't be better than finding you."

"It is." And then Joan told him the news from León. "You can go back to Nicaragua whenever you want to now."

Juan glanced at Maura. "I'll have to think about that," he said.

Chapter Thirty-Three

Seamus
Hudson, New York
March 1993

Seamus felt deeply satisfied in having pulled off the celebration for Caitlin and Malika, and, by chance, the reunion of Joan and Juan. He asked Maura why she'd been so quiet about her friendship with Juan, and she told him about Terrance's impending visit plans and Juan's not wanting to interfere with her marriage. That made Seamus like him all the more. Juan was gentle and firm with Ben and Toby, and it was easy to see that they thrived in his company. Maura too had a glow about her. Seamus had also been impressed by Juan's efficiency in setting up a computer system for the bookstore. One Saturday when Seamus was working at his desk near the children's section, and Juan came upstairs to look for a book, Seamus asked him in Spanish, "Would you be able to find me a second-hand computer and install it up here? I can't make head nor tail of computers, but my partner, Jasmine, is a whizz on them, and I think it would make things more efficient for her."

Juan answered him in Spanish, "Of course. I would be happy to. And if you would want me to, I could show you how to use it. You might find it made things more efficient for you as well."

Seamus gave a short laugh and then said, "No thanks. Jasmine tried to show me. I was worse than all thumbs. Paper and pencil is how is I like to record information."

Juan said in a more formal tone of voice, "There is something else that I would appreciate talking with you about. May I join you for a minute?"

"Sure, sit down. What's on your mind?"

After sitting in one of the client chairs, Juan said, "Maura told me that you and your wife took care of her after her father died. I look to you as representing her father. Is that right?"

"Yes, in a way. Maura's father was my best friend as well as my brother-in-law. Maura's mother died in childbirth. When her father died, Maura begged her grandparents to let her live with me and Rose. She was only with us about a year and a half before she left to go to college in England. But they were good years and we loved her as our own. So yes, you could say that in some ways I represent her father."

"Maura showed me a letter from her husband in England. He told her that he wanted a divorce. He also wrote her that he did not want to see his sons until they were old enough to travel on their own."

"Yes, Maura told me about that."

"Because her husband has written that letter, and because Maura has told me that she also wants a divorce from her husband, I want to say to you, Señor Seamus, that Maura and Toby and Ben make me happy to be alive every day!"

"Well then," Seamus responded after a moment, "If Maura feels the same, I hope things work out well for the four of you."

"I am very grateful that you say that to me!" Juan said.

Seamus thought that if he was representing Maura's father, he should ask Juan about his prospects.

"Are you liking your job doing maintenance at the school?"

"The people I work with are all good to me and generous. They have to teach me as we go along. My only work experience before I came to the States was with computers. I'm trying to get my English fluent enough so that I can repair and sell them in Hudson."

"Perhaps meanwhile you could give lessons in Spanish to people wanting to know more about computers. Jasmine and I could add your name to our list of resources for local immigrants."

"Thank you, that would be very helpful. And thank you again for being open to my talking with you about Maura and the boys."

The next morning Seamus received a letter from Maggie. The envelope had more stamps than usual which made it look like express mail.

"*Dear Seamus,*

I'm in great difficulty. My daughter Hannah's husband has left her. Their son, Michael, seems to think that Hannah and I are the reason that his father has left. He has become aggressive — kicking and biting if we get close enough, while cursing and shouting that we're hurting him. He's thirteen, big for his age, and strong!

We made the mistake of thinking that taking a trip after his father left would be a good distraction. We're in a small hotel in New Delhi and we're eager to get home to Bombay so we can get help for him. But Michael now refuses to leave the hotel!

My son is traveling in China and unreachable. Seamus, would you consider the possibility of joining us here in New Delhi and helping us get Michael home? Maura has plenty of money to cover your tickets in our business account. I will completely understand, Seamus, if you're not able to do this, but if you can't come, could you send me suggestions for what I should do?

With good wishes for you always, Maggie

Seamus called Jasmine and read Maggie's letter aloud. Her response was immediate, "Seamus, we can hire an interpreter while you're gone. Please tell Maggie how grateful I am about her letting us work out of the book store. Tell me what time your plane goes, and Gordon and I will drive you to the Hartford Airport."

Chapter Thirty-Four

Joan
Boston
March 1993

Joan decided to stop working at Hillside Orchards once Juan was found safe, happy, and in love. Continuing to work there seemed to be clinging to a purpose that no longer existed. Another goal, being as close as possible to Sarah and her family, also seemed less necessary. Sarah and Joe were busy in their full-time jobs, and Sam and Kari wanted to spend weekends at the Academy doing projects and playing games with other faculty children who had become close friends.

Joan was happy for them all, although a little wistful about her grandchildren. She had hugely enjoyed their weekends together. Her lack of purpose made her feel confused and a little at a loss. She realized she would have to create her own path.

When Caleb asked Joan to join him in Boston for a few days, "Please come help me explore future hometown possibilities for after retirement," Joan agreed immediately. She was happy for a distraction from her confusion.

They met at South Station, Joan having come to Boston by bus, and Caleb taking the subway from the airport. It was windy and rainy, and they took a taxi to the Beacon Hotel to drop their bags. Then they headed off to visit Paul Revere's House, Quincy Market, and the Gardner Museum.

That evening, tired, and with their minds filled with wonderful imagery, they rested together on the balcony outside Joan's room. The rain and wind had stopped, and they lay side by side on lounge chairs with blankets from their two bedrooms covering them cozily as they looked up at the sky bright with stars. They talked softly into the cold sharp listening darkness.

"On good days retiring feels like an adventure," Caleb said. "On bad days it feels like sliding down a slippery slope."

"I know what you mean. For me that's true of widowhood. Sometimes I feel even a bit excited about creating a new life on my own. At other times I'm simply waiting to die so Oscar and I can be together again."

"Isn't that the truth! It amazes me, Joanie, how well we've understood each other all these years."

After a few minutes Joan asked, "Does Boston feel like a place where you'd like to live? Do you have friends here?"

"I have you and Sarah a few hours away. Maybe I should move closer to all of you."

"Would you miss city life."

"Do you miss it?"

"Sometimes."

"Could you imagine moving back to Boston?"

"I don't think so. I don't know anyone here now."

"If I were here, you'd know me."

Joan didn't know how to reply to that, so she just stared at the stars.

After a few minutes Caleb said, "I know you want to be near Sarah and the kids, but if we lived here together, I could run you down there as often as you liked. And we could have Sam and Kari up here to introduce them to city life."

"I'm not sure what you're saying," Joan said, although she sort of was.

"No wonder. I'm not saying it well." There was another few moments of silence, and then Caleb continued, "You and I have been friends for more than half a century; perhaps we should consider spending the rest of our lives together?" He reached for Joan's hand under the blankets.

Joan stared up into the darkness; clouds covered, uncovered, and then covered the stars again. She knew Caleb. He was courageous and wise. He would take good care of her. He was the first man she'd been in love with, although he'd only had eyes for Marianne. She lay there, hand in hand with Caleb, wondering — perhaps she need not speak at all. Perhaps she could say yes by saying nothing.

But Joan didn't want to be passive in her life. Life with Oscar had been filled with colors, the red of passion, the yellow of the blazing sunlight that she'd learned to take her hat off to, and the blue of the precious water that arrived at their house infrequently and in small quantities. When Oscar and his children left to fight the Contras, Joan had continued to live passionately, studying Spanish intensely, so that when the family returned they could talk freely, and making friends with her neighbors as they helped each other through the anguish of being left at home while the people they loved were fighting in the mountains.

Joan knew that Caleb wasn't in love with her, nor would ever be. He was in love with her sister. "I don't think I'm ready for that," she said finally, not knowing how long she'd made Caleb wait for her answer.

She was not sure of what she was going to say next. Caleb still held her hand, warm, strong, caring. Perhaps his hand surrounding hers helped her to hear her own thoughts and put them into words. "I feel as though I'm still married to Oscar. Now that Juan is safe and happy, and in no hurry to go home, I think I'll go back to our house in Malpisillo. I miss the neighbors popping in and out of each other's houses, the children playing games on every street, and the volcano looking over us day and night. I think I'm going to go home."

"What about Sarah and the children?"

"They're all doing well, busy and happy in their lives. They can come visit when they like. I think I left Nicaragua too precipitously. Malpaisillo was my home during the war. I want to experience it in peace time. It was my home when I was in love. I want to experience it as a widow. The people there welcomed me when I couldn't speak their language. I want to experience my neighbors now that I can understand and discuss whatever subject comes up."

"May I come and visit you there?"

"Yes, of course. We'd go into León and explore. It's a beautiful city."

His hand still held hers. Her pleasure in his warmth quickened her determination to live on her own, to really be Oscar's widow, before she explored other possibilities.

Chapter Thirty-Five

Maura
Treehouse Books
April 1993

The third Saturday in April was Juan's birthday. Maura closed the bookstore early, filled a basket with sandwiches, drinks, and cupcakes decorated by the boys, and the four of them climbed the hill behind the bookstore. They were following a path that Juan and the boys had discovered when they were looking for animal tracks. Birds called back and forth as the shadows lengthened. At a rocky outcropping with a wide view, they unpacked the basket, ate and drank, sang happy birthday to Juan, and pointed out birds and deer to each other. When they were satiated, the boys went exploring. Juan and Maura sat together leaning their backs against the same tree.

"I need go to León," Juan said quietly. "Not stay long, but need go."

"I will miss you. We'll all miss you. It has been wonderful

having you here. I can't tell you how much..." Maura's legs trembled slightly as she spoke.

"What I like is work with computers. You know that. Until I speak English good I no can work here with computers."

"Perhaps you could study English more intensely. Perhaps I could give you lessons, actual lessons, not like the kids."

"Yes, that is good. But now I need travel to León. I need talk with owner of store."

"Oh, Juan," was all Maura could say.

"I come back, Maura," he said and reached for her hand. Ben and Toby came running towards them. "We saw a fox! a real fox!" Ben shouted.

"It was light brown all over except for white in some places. It looked at us, really looked, before it ran away," Toby added.

"That's wonderful," Maura said listlessly despite herself. "Why don't you show Juan where the fox was — maybe you'll see his den, while I pack up the basket. Then please come right back; it's time we headed down."

That evening when Juan left to drive back to Hudson, Maura wondered if she would ever see him again.

The next morning Maura set her card table desk up in front of the bookstore. The sun was warming the world up, and customers were talking happily inside. Maura opened the two letters she'd forgotten to take out of the mail box the day before.

The first was from Maggie.

Dear Maura,

We never talked about what would happen after this summer. You've been a terrific store manager! You've made important improvements, and if things were different I would ask you to continue for as long as you wanted.

But a difficulty has arisen. My daughter, Hannah, will be coming home with me, and she's bringing her son, Michael, who needs special care. They're going to have to live in your apartment, and she wants to work at the store as her way of paying rent.

Please understand, Maura, that although I'm delighted in many ways to have Hannah and Michael live with me, I'm extremely sad and sorry that I can't employ you as well. Your organized, creative, and welcoming management of the bookstore has been a huge help to the store as well as to me. I am enclosing a rave reference for you to copy and send to anyone who asks for it.

Big Hugs of Gratitude and Affection, Maggie!

ps: Your uncle Seamus helped me hugely by coming here. He's wonderful with Michael who seems to trust him more than anyone else. We're going to do our best to home-school Michael, and I'm hoping that having Seamus and Jasmine working upstairs will help Michael adjust to being there.

I'll let you know when we're coming. Seamus says to tell you he's looking forward to having you and the boys live with him in Hudson until you decide what you're going to do next. Once we get back, I will, of course, continue to give you twenty-five percent of whatever the store takes in, until September.

Maura put the letter and the enclosed reference on the table and leaned back against the wall of the bookstore. Once again, she realized, she'd been asleep at the wheel. As her joy in Juan's company became stronger and stronger, and as the boys made friends and did well in school and day care, she'd stopped sending out applications to colleges. She'd figured she would just stay at the bookstore, without ever questioning if that would be possible, and without thinking that Juan might leave for Nicaragua. She had also slowed way down working on her book. It was not ready enough to try to sell it to a publisher and ask for an advance. It was kind of Seamus to offer to take them in, but it wouldn't work for more than a few weeks because his apartment was so small.

Maura closed her eyes, leaned back against the wall, tipped her face into the sun's full warmth and light, and tried to breathe deeply. She felt like Atlas being made to carry the world on her shoulders against her will.

After a few minutes, or many, she was not really sure, she opened the second letter. It was an express mail from Terrance.

Dearest Maura,

Your foolish husband has once again been made a fool of. I wish I had the wisdom of King Lear's fool. Yesterday Carlotta married a wealthy French film star almost twice her age.

I, on the other hand, have just signed an excellent three-year contract for a new soap opera! I realize how difficult it must have been for you to support us between shows. I'm going to work harder, and I've told my agent he has to work harder to make my downtimes shorter. I have a reputation as a charismatic, skillful, hard-working actor, and there's no reason why I can't support my family, even as the boys get older and want to go to prep school and university.

I love you, Maura. Always have. You know that. I beg you to forgive me my many mistakes and stupidities, "early onset middle-age madness" I call it. I've gotten the craziness out of my system once and for all.

I beg you to consider the life and love we have shared and our sons' happiness. Could you, please dearest Maura, find it in your heart to forgive me? With this new contract I can support us while you get the PhD you deserve. You'll have time to finish your book and make it your thesis! Please let me help you with your career the way you have so wonderfully helped me!

Please think about all this and come at least for a long visit so Mum and I can spend time with you and the boys, and you and I can talk everything over. I'm enclosing a money order to cover first class tickets!

All my Love, Terrance

Maura folded the letters and put them in her jeans pocket. It was too much to think about while the boys were awake. Toby and Ben came back from the farm at lunch time bringing their friends. Leaving a sign at the store for customers to come by the house if they wanted to pay for books, Maura quickly heated up some soup, and made a plate of sandwiches. For desert the children finished off the brownies that Toby and

Ben had helped her bake the night before. Maura went back to the store and enjoyed hearing the five children play hide and seek in the woods behind the house.

After closing the bookstore that afternoon, Maura walked with the boys back to the farm to watch the cows be brought in from the fields to be milked. The seven cows each went to the same stall morning and afternoon. Two agricultural students did the milking by hand. While the boys played outside, Maura found herself becoming very still and almost calm as she watched the cows patiently waiting their turns.

That evening as the boys shared a bath, Maura overheard Ben ask Toby, "Do you think he'll come?"

"I don't know," Toby said.

She wondered if they were talking about Terrance? Would she be harming Ben and Toby in some way by not reuniting with their father? Where would they live now, and how would she support them? Was Juan really coming back?

Chapter Thirty-Six

Joan
Malpaisillo, Nicaragua
May 1993

Joan had foreseen that she would be lonely at times in Malpaisillo. During the war she'd made friends among the neighbors whose husbands and children were fighting against the Contras. In those days she'd assumed Oscar and his children would return when the fighting was done. Now she was feeling a different kind of loneliness. She hoped it would change into courage or determination or even joy in life itself.

She swept the hard-earth floor each morning and walked to the market for groceries, stopping along the way to chat with neighbors. Her favorite part of the day was the afternoons which she spent at the library. Families who couldn't afford school fees sent their children to the library.

Joan read aloud to the younger children and helped the older children read aloud to her. She loved experiencing the moment when a child realized that he or she was actually reading, no longer just remembering.

In the evenings Joan sewed, read, or wrote letters, sometimes including drawings she made of the volcano or a neighbor's donkey, or a child learning to read. Sam and Kari responded with drawings of their own which she tacked up on the walls and enjoyed catching glimpses of during the day.

One morning on a day when she was feeling particularly alone, Joan received a letter from Juan in Spanish.

Dearest Juana,

Believe it or not, Maura's crazy ex-husband decided he wanted to be married to her again. Without telling Maura he was coming, he flew to Albany, and called her at the store to come pick him up. I was still in León at the time.

Maura took him back to the bookstore; what else could she do? The boys were thrilled to see their father of course. He threw his money around, buying them toys and begging Maura to return to England with him.

Luckily, he had a job in England he had to get back for, so two days later he left. When I got back from León, the boys were in a state of complete confusion, you can imagine, and Maura looked as though she'd been run over by a truck.

I wondered at first if it was possible that Maura wished she hadn't signed the divorce papers last winter and wanted now to return to England. But then she showed me a letter from Maggie ending her job at the bookstore. After I read it, she said, 'I don't know now where we'll live, or how I'll support the boys!'

That's when I told her about the job I'd just obtained at a big computer store in León. I begged that she and the boys would move to Nicaragua with me and that she would become my wife. We both cried and laughed a little when she said yes. She'd been afraid I wouldn't return to the States from Nicaragua, and I'd been afraid that she was in love with her ex again and would be leaving for England. We took the boys for a walk and told them our plans, and it was as though all their confusion about their father's visit fell away. The four of us took hands and walked down the empty road singing Christmas carols in both Spanish and English at the same time.

In terms of the wedding, we can't get married in a Catholic church even if I were willing to convert, because of Maura's divorce. I no longer feel connected to Papa's church, but I do feel close to Papa's friend, Reverend Gomez, who retired a few years ago. We plan to ask Reverend Gomez if he would be willing to marry us in the park in Malpaisillo.

I didn't call you when I was in León about the job because I was in a great rush to get back to Maura. My salary will support all four of us if we live simply. Maura will take Spanish classes at the University. Her plan is to quickly learn enough Spanish so she can get a job at the University or at a high school teaching English Literature. Meanwhile she'll finish her book.

We could live in an apartment in León, but what would you think of our living with you? I'd love for Toby and Ben to be able to go to my old school in Malpaisillo. Maura and I could take the bus into León each day. If that's possible for you, we would much prefer it. The boys have become so accustomed to the freedom of living in the country that we're loath to close them up in a city apartment again, the way they were in London.

I know we're asking a lot. Not only would we be crowding you, but we'd be asking you to keep an eye on the boys until we came back each evening. We would understand completely if you would rather live by yourself for a while. In that case we would get an apartment in León and visit you when you wanted us to on weekends.

Please let us know what you think. Either way, it will be wonderful living together again in Nicaragua, and giving the children such a wonderful grandmother.

hugs and kisses, Juan

Joan folded the letter into her pocket and walked, as quickly as she could, downtown to the Mayor's office to ask for special permission to use their phone. The Mayor wasn't there. His secretary, Maria, took one look at Joan's face, and pushed the phone toward her, saying "as quick as you can because he'll be coming in shortly."

Joan sent an air kiss to Maria as she asked the long-distance operator for the number. She was calling Juan at his job and spoke in rapid Spanish. "Please live with me. Imagine how happy your papa will be to know we are all together."

His reply was a little breathless, "Wonderful! Thank you. That makes everything perfect. I'll write you soon about...." But then the phone went dead, as it often did. In this case it was good timing because the Mayor entered, greeted Joan with a smile and a peck on the cheek, and asked Maria to come into his office for dictation. Joan left some money on

Maria's desk for the phone bill, and, feeling like Gene Kelly in the rain, she danced herself back out onto the street under the shining sun.

Chapter Thirty-Seven

Seamus
Hudson, New York
June 1993

Jasmine went to the airport to meet the plane from Bombay. When she brought everyone to Treehouse Books, they found Maura and the boys had packed their car and were ready to leave. "Uncle Seamus, we're going to stay with you for two nights!" Toby told him.

"Then we're going to Nicaragua!" Ben explained, carefully pronouncing the word.

Seamus gave them big hugs and introduced them to Hannah and Michael. Michael immediately got out the wooden puppet that Seamus had given him. It had strings attached to all the joints which were manipulated from a cross of two sticks that Michael held. He had been practicing for many hours how to make the puppet shake hands, bow, and even dance. He now climbed up onto the bench in front of the bookstore and performed what he had learned. Ben and Toby were in awe, asking for many encores. Michael beamed with pleasure and pride. Maggie sighed and gave Seamus a kiss on the cheek. Hannah turned from her son's smile to hide a tear.

"If you have a minute," Maura said to Maggie. "I want to give you a quick tour of the bookstore before I leave, because I've moved things around a bit."

Hannah joined them on the tour, "Might as well jump right in."

When they were back outdoors, Maggie said, "You've done wonders. Not only is the store making more money, but I've been getting letters from people, especially from old bookseller friends in the city, praising your purchasing choices and saying how wonderful you are to work with."

Seamus noticed Hannah turn away as her mother praised Maura. He put his arm around her shoulders, and said, "Let's go in the kitchen and see if there's anything to eat." There was. Maura had filled the refrigerator with a roast chicken, a green salad, and a potato salad, as well as vanilla ice cream and brownies.

When they all were happily full, with hugs all around and a few tears, Seamus drove Maura, Ben and Toby to his apartment in Hudson.

He spent the next two days with them. They went to the Firemen's Museum where the boys were allowed to a climb up into the fire trucks and pretend to steer them. They went bowling and applauded when Toby managed to get a strike.

And they went to see a local baseball game. Very early the next morning Seamus drove them to Kennedy Airport. He gave Maura a rosary that had belonged to Rose, and he gave each of the boys a silver dollar. He hated watching them disappear into the crowd as they went through security.

That afternoon he went back to work at the bookstore. Juan had set up a computer and phone system on the second floor. Maura had shelved books in Spanish near their desk. Jasmine had left a note that she was on a transportation run. Since many of their clients did not have cars, Jasmine and Seamus took turns bringing them to and from the bookstore. Seamus listened to the messages on the answering machine and began to answer calls.

Chapter Thirty-Eight

Maura
Malpaisillo, Nicaragua
June — September 1993

At the Managua airport, Juan squatted down to hug Ben and Toby as they ran to him. Then he straightened up and put his arms around Maura who felt as though she'd come home, despite being in such a new environment. He drove them to Malpaisillo where Joan gave them a warm welcome and a tour of the house. She'd made colorful quilts, for the bunks Juan had bought for the boys' room, and for the double bed in the largest bedroom. Maura beamed at Joan and sighed with pleasure as she realized how truly happy Joan was to be sharing her house with them.

After lunch, Juan left to take the car back to his friend in León. He told Maura he would need to work late but would come in to say "Good night" before everyone went to bed. He was staying with a friend across town until the wedding.

Joan said to the boys, "I think it's best if you begin school tomorrow. We can walk over there now. The children will have left, but you can meet the teachers. It's only three blocks from here."

Toby asked, "What will happen if we don't understand what they're telling us to do?"

"That's an excellent question," Joan said. "That's what we'll ask the teachers this afternoon." As the four of them walked toward the school, Ben took Maura's hand and then Toby took Joan's hand. Maura smiled at him, realizing that Toby didn't want Joan to feel left out.

Toby's first grade teacher, who looked old enough to have many grandchildren, asked Toby with very clear gestures to help her bring a desk and chair from another room and place them in the front row.

When Joan repeated Toby's question, she smiled at him, shrugged her shoulders and said, "We make best try." Maura could see Toby relax and smile in relief.

In Ben's kindergarten room the walls were cheery with children's drawings on large newsprint sheets. The teacher handed Ben and Toby thumbtacks so they could help her pin them up. Joan and Maura watched as the young teacher and the boys had fun trying to make the drawings straight — with lots of gestures and a good deal of laughter.

As they walked home Maura asked the boys what they thought about the school. "You know, Mum," Toby said, "I don't think you need to walk with us tomorrow. I will hold

Ben's hand until we get to his room. Then I'll go to my room. I think it might look better if we go to school on our own."

"What do you think of that idea, Ben?" Maura asked, somewhat surprised.

"Good."

"What do you think, Joan?"

"I think they'll be fine." The boys looked delighted by her answer. She added, "I'll give them each a piece of paper in their lunch baskets saying the names of their teachers, in case someone asks. My guess is that you boys will pick up Spanish very quickly."

Joan was right. The boys made friends their first day at the school, and immediately learned the words they needed to play various outdoor games during recess and on the streets after school. A few weeks later, Toby's teacher said that he was one of the fastest at adding numbers, and Ben's teacher praised his ability to recite with everyone whether or not he understood the words. "Comprehension will come very soon," she told Joan.

Maura and Juan took the bus to León each morning. Juan was enjoying his job immensely. He was called "Doctor" by his colleagues because he was able to fix computers that everyone else had given up on.

Maura spent her days at the University. She signed up for a class on the History of North American Literature. This was the kind of class she would like to be teaching when she was fluent in Spanish. The class was taught in Spanish but the students were reading excerpts from books in English. After the first class, Maura introduced herself to the professor, Señorita Gomez, who spoke English with a Nicaraguan accent, and immediately invited Maura to have coffee with her. "I am thrilled to have you in my class. Would you consider sometimes reading aloud for the class? It would be wonderful for my students to hear how these writings should really sound. We will be studying Nathaniel Hawthorne, Edgar Allen Poe, Emily Dickinson, Herman Melville, Walt Whitman, and Henry James. Do you know them?"

Maura smiled, "I know them well."

"That is wonderful. I am writing my PhD thesis on Poe's stories. Perhaps you would consider letting me talk with you about them some day." Then after a minute she said, "I wonder what I could do for you in exchange?"

"What about giving me Spanish lessons?" Maura said.

"Excellent idea, Spanish and coffee after class." Margarita Gomez became Maura's first friend in Nicaragua.

Chapter Thirty-Nine

Joan
Malpaisillo, Nicaragua
October 1993

Juan and Maura decided on October 21st as the date for the wedding. They arranged with the retired Evangelical minister Reverend Gomez, who had known Juan all his life, to have the ceremony in the park. Maura confided to Joan that she found herself wishing she could talk with a Catholic priest about it all.

"Father Perez is the Catholic priest here." Joan told her. "He's an elderly mild-mannered Jesuit, not at all judgmental. He speaks English. I'm sure you'll like him."

When they visited Father Perez and Maura told him her story, he said, "I would be honored to bless your union with Juan, either at the time of your wedding or later. Your children are always welcome at our Sunday school, and if our Lord is present for you in the sanctified bread and wine, then please share communion with us."

Maura told Joan as they walked home, "I look forward to introducing Uncle Seamus to Father Perez. He's a lot like Father Brennan whom we all loved. It felt almost as though Aunt Rose was standing beside him nodding at me in agreement with everything he said."

They sent out invitations to the family in the States.

Please bring yourselves, not presents, to Nicaragua
Help us Celebrate and Rejoice in the marriage of
Juan Estrada and Maura Trowbridge
in the Malpaisillo town park
Wednesday, October 21st
11:00 am

When everyone agreed to come, including Maggie and her grandson, Michael, Joan began asking her friends for suggestions for where she could lodge her overflow guests. The Mayor offered three rooms, "Your husband was a close friend, and my house is your house for this happy celebration."

On the morning of the wedding all the northerners gathered at Joan's house for a festive breakfast. Those who had spent the night with neighbors told happy stories about the families they'd boarded with — Joan realized how generously her neighbors had welcomed her friends and family into their homes.

After breakfast the wedding party strolled to the park at the center of town, where they met Juan, their neighbors, Juan's friends from León, Father Perez and Reverend Gomez. Joan thought they looked like a flock of many colored birds. The men were handsome in blue or grey light-weight suits, or in colorfully embroidered white shirts over white pants. The women wore dresses of all the colors of the rainbow. Joan had made Maura's dress, white with yellow trim around the neckline, waist and hem. Maura wore a pearl necklace that Veronica, her former mother-in-law, had sent her. "We're still the best of friends," Maura told Joan.

Caleb and some friends of Juan's were setting up rows of folding chairs that had been borrowed from the school. Joan's son-in-law, Joe, began to play a ditty on his oboe to tell people it was time to find a chair because the ceremony was about to start. Just as people were deciding where to sit, a clap of thunder made everyone look up, and heavy rain began to pour down on their faces. Father Perez shouted out, "The Catholic church is just across the street. Please do us the honor."

"Thank you, Father!" people called to him. Joan noticed that the northerners hunched their shoulders and quickly ran towards the church for shelter, while many of the Nicaraguans laughed with pleasure at the rain. Some of them stood stock still for a minute with their arms held wide and their faces turned to the sky in a gesture of welcoming and gratitude.

Soon though, they were all gathered in the church. Father Perez and Reverend Gomez conferred at one side of the church. They both wore collars but no robes. After a few moments, they shook hands, and Reverend Gomez went to stand in front of the altar.

Seamus and Maura waited in the back of the church with Kari, Toby, and Ben, who had baskets of confetti to sprinkle along the center aisle. Michael had been invited to join them but preferred to sit with Maggie. Sam held a small cushion with two wedding rings.

Joe with his oboe and Malika with a lyre from Kenya stood near the altar and played a duet that Joe had composed for the occasion. Then at a sign from Reverend Gomez, they began to play their arrangement of Mendelssohn's wedding march. Everyone stood, and the procession began.

The younger children led, spreading colorful confetti. Then came Sam, with one hand held over the cushion to ensure that the rings didn't slip off. Finally, Maura came smiling down the aisle with her hand in the crook of Seamus's arm. From the front of the church Juan beamed at her as though she were a lighthouse in a raging storm.

When they arrived at the altar Juan and Maura faced Reverend Gomez with the children on either side of them. Reverend Gomez asked in Spanish, "Who gives this woman in marriage?"

Seamus answered in Spanish, "It is my honor to do so." He kissed Maura on the cheek and turned to sit down next to Maggie and Michael. The children stayed standing, but Joe and Malika went to sit beside Sarah and Caitlin.

Reverend Gomez began by thanking Father Perez for his hospitality. Then the ceremony began. Reverend Gomez had warned Maura that he would have to do the ceremony in Spanish because his English was so limited. But it looked to Joan as though Maura was understanding everything that was being said. She remembered her own marriage to Oscar when she knew almost no Spanish. The resonance of the ceremony had spoken to her as clearly as though she'd understood the words. She and Oscar had had their own unspoken language, and she realized that Juan and Maura had the same, although they were both working hard at being able to speak fluently in each other's languages. They had planned on speaking English at home for the sake of the boys, but the boys could already speak Spanish more comfortably than Maura, so now Spanish had become the home language.

Joan had taught Maura the words to say in Spanish when she and Juan exchanged rings and they promised to have and to hold each other no matter what until they were parted by death. She saw Maura become pale for a moment as she said the words and wondered if it was because Maura was fearful of forgetting them, of if she had momentarily thought of Terrance, whom she had not stayed with. Her color revived a moment later as she and Juan were pronounced man and wife, and Juan kissed her robustly to everyone's applause. Reverend Gomez, in his very limited English, tried to explain to the non-Spanish speakers what the ceremony had involved. He quickly had them all laughing as he tried to pantomime the English words he didn't know. Then he invited Father Perez to come forward. Father Perez gathered Ben and Toby in front of Maura and Juan; he held his hands above their heads and recited prayers in both Spanish and English. It seemed to Joan that Father Perez's prayers were like rain falling on parched ground, both essential and miraculous.

At a sign from Reverend Gomez, Joe returned to the front of the church where he faced the congregation and began to sing a song he'd learned while living in Nicaragua that described the wonders of the country. Juan and his Nicaraguan friends started singing with Joe so heartily that the North Americans joined in on the choruses, despite not understanding the words. As everyone sang, Juan and Maura and the children led their families and friends in a procession to the back of the church and through the large opened doors into the misty sunshine, which was enhanced now by a double rainbow.

May Paddock

Acknowledgments

Winslow Eliot, my sister, made this book possible with her encouragement, her insightful and sometimes radical suggestions, and her editorial knowhow. Tom Stier, my brother-in-law, created the form of the book and the cover. Kendell Shaffer, my sister-in-law, gave me essential editorial advice. I am blessed to be surrounded by a family that is not only supportive but knowledgeable and willing to critique what I've done. Rosemary Ahern edited this book and encouraged me all along the way; she kept me afloat when I thought the ship was sinking. Tom Hahn gave me a helpful critique, and Leslie Wood gave me a great boost of encouragement and support for both my books. Thank you all!

May Paddock

About the Author

After retiring from teaching high school, May Paddock worked with migrant farm workers, advocating for them, interpreting, and teaching English. This is her second novel, a continuation of the story in *Surprised by Love*. She lives in Upstate New York.

www.ingramcontent.com/pod-product-compliance
Lightning Source LLC
Chambersburg PA
CBHW031330170626
46807CB00002B/628